"Your cousin was blackmailing someone."

Eversleigh kept his voice low and discreet. "And the proof is somewhere in this house."

"Then you think our intruder last night was connected?" said Hester calmly.

"I'm afraid so," confirmed Eversleigh.

Hester rose. "I appreciate your confiding in me, but it still does not alter my decision. I intend to stay."

Lord Eversleigh stood beside her. "Your attitude may be admirable, Miss Martingale, but it is also extremely foolish. Whatever knowledge your cousin possessed very likely cost him his life."

"I understand that, sir. You've made it quite clear."

"Have I also made it clear, Miss Martingale, that if you persist in remaining here, against my advice, your own life may be in danger?"

A TOUCH OF BLACKMAIL

JEANNE CARMICHAEL

Harlequin Books

TORONTO • NEW YORK • LONDON
AMSTERDAM • PARIS • SYDNEY • HAMBURG
STOCKHOLM • ATHENS • TOKYO • MILAN

For my Mother, Jean A. Stitz
with deepest love and gratitude
for all her understanding and
endless patience. And especially
for sharing with me her love of books.

Published August 1991

ISBN 0-373-31156-7

A TOUCH OF BLACKMAIL

CHAPTER ONE

HESTER MARTINGALE hesitantly entered the offices of Rundle and Rundle, Solicitors. The clerk looked up briefly, but once a quick assessment had convinced him that she was no one to take trouble over, he returned to his paperwork without speaking. Hester, wishing she were taller than her five and a half feet, approached the desk. In her best schoolroom voice, she announced, "I am Miss Martingale, and I am here at the request of Mr. Rundle concerning a legacy."

The clerk eyed her dispassionately. A tall, scrawny fellow with a blemished face and dirty fingernails, he still presumed to judge others by their appearance. On occasion he could be conciliatory, almost obsequious, in his attentions. Now, however, he dismissed Miss Martingale with contempt, rating her no better than a dowdy governess. Only her mention of a legacy prevented him from treating her with outright rudeness. He stirred himself sufficiently to direct her to a hard wooden bench where she might have a seat while she waited.

"Mr. Rundle's with his lordship. When he's done, then mayhap he'll see you."

Hester nodded and settled down to wait, fingering the letter she had received from the solicitor. She wished he had written in more detail. The letter told her very little, other than an unknown cousin had died and that, as his last living relative, she would inherit his estate. Mr. Rundle had added a cautionary note that there might be very little left after all her cousin's debts were discharged.

Hester returned the creased and much-folded letter to her reticule and made an effort to tidy herself. The stagecoach had been crowded, and extremely dusty. Her travelling dress was sadly stained, and she knew the dark brown colour was not becoming to her. As she adjusted the wide-brimmed hat she wore, she felt its single feather dangling limply. It had become crushed when she had tried to nap in the coach. Perhaps, she thought optimistically, her bequest would be enough to enable her to replenish her wardrobe. She whiled away the tedium of waiting by imagining the various ensembles she might purchase.

It wasn't long before she chided herself for her vanity, for Hester believed that no matter how well she might dress, she would always be considered rather plain. She was not the sort of lady who attracted undue attention. She had no notion that her large brown eyes and the warmth of her smile were universally appealing. As for her nose, she discounted it as a shabby little thing which tilted absurdly upwards—not at all in the long, straight style of accredited beauties.

She brought her mind back to the present as the oak door opposite the railing opened, and two gentlemen stepped out. The first was obviously the lord the clerk had mentioned. Hester forgot her own discomfort as she studied the handsome creature before her. She guessed he was only a few years older than herself, but *he* was elegantly dressed, although not in the modish style affected by the dandies she had seen during her one London Season. His coat appeared simply cut, but she noted the way it fit snugly across his wide shoulders, and she knew intuitively that it was an expensive garment. Her eyes travelled down the long length of him and took in his buff pantaloons, which almost seemed moulded to a fine pair of muscular legs—no need for padding there. And she could almost see her reflection in his highly polished Hessian boots. As her eyes came up slowly and encountered his, she was appalled to realize that the young man was watching her.

A tinge of pink in her cheeks showed her obvious chagrin at being caught in such rudeness, and she hastily looked away.

The clerk scrambled forward to hold open the door, bowing and smiling inanely. ''His lordship'' ignored him and turned to shake hands with the older gentleman. Hester dared to steal another peep at him, and found his eyes still watching her. He grinned and nodded in her direction as he left.

Hester had scant time to be embarrassed. The clerk made her presence known, and Mr. Rundle crossed the room to greet her warmly. He was rather tall, but his shoulders were stooped with age, and the white hair and whiskers he wore gave him a benevolent look. He kept her hand in his as he guided her into his office, and saw her comfortably seated before a large, cluttered desk. The solicitor seated himself, and searching amid the large stack of papers that seemed to cover his desk, he pulled out the very one he wanted. Adjusting his spectacles, he peered at her.

''Now, Miss Martingale, let me first offer you my condolences on the death of your cousin.''

Her smile came readily. ''Thank you, but you see, I never knew Stuart Martingale, or even that I *had* a cousin. Can you tell me what he was like, or anything about him?''

"A most unfortunate young man. Most unfortunate. I'm afraid I didn't know him well. It was his father, Cyrus, whom I knew, and he was a fine gentleman. I believe if he had lived longer, matters might have been different. Sadly, he suffered an early death and young Stuart came into his inheritance when he was just turned eighteen. Too young, perhaps, to handle his responsibilities. Squandered most of his wealth, I'm afraid, and let his lands go to seed. He never would listen to any advice. The boy was addicted to drink, and always ready to lay down a wager. He played fairly deep when it came to cards, and luck didn't favour him. Apparently, he got in over his head and was forced to sell off everything that wasn't entailed. His neighbour, Lord Eversleigh, picked up most of the deeds, and now he owns all of the surrounding land. All that's left to you of Silverdale, I regret to say, is the house itself, and a few acres. And even that is in disrepair."

"And is that my inheritance? The house and the few acres?"

The solicitor sighed. "It is, and it isn't. Allow me to explain. Last year Stuart came to me and requested that I find a buyer for Silverdale. I suggested Lord Eversleigh, naturally, since he already owns the surrounding acreage, but Stuart wouldn't have it. He flew into a rage, Miss Martingale, and even accused Eversleigh of trying to ruin him. It's utter nonsense, of course, but there you are. I promised I'd see what I could do, and then, only a month later, Stuart wrote me that he wouldn't be selling the house, after all. He said he came into some money, and I do know he paid off some of his more pressing creditors."

"I see. Where did his windfall come from?"

"Wouldn't tell me! And therein lies our problem. Stuart was receiving a tidy sum every month, but there's no record where it came from, and no way of knowing if it will continue. I shall have to journey down there and go through his papers before we can determine the extent of your legacy."

Hester felt uneasy. The palms of her hands grew damp, and she tried not to show her anxiety. "Then it will be some time before I shall know? Or receive anything?" Her voice didn't betray her, but Rundle easily read the worry in her eyes.

"You are distressed! I'm sorry, but you must understand that such things take time. I'm sure it will be no more than a month or two before everything is resolved."

"A month or two! Oh, dear. I had hoped I could go to the estate at once. You see, when I received your letter, I asked Mrs. Thadge-Morton to allow me a holiday to come up to London. She... she refused, and I'm afraid my deplorable temper got the better of me. I gave notice. I know I should not have acted so rashly, but it was quite unbearable there in any case. She would *not* allow her children to be disciplined.... I'm sorry, I didn't mean to run on like this."

He looked at her sympathetically. "Yes, I rather see your problem. Well, if you really wish it, I see no reason why you could not stay at Silverdale until everything is settled. And I shall advance you a small sum to tide you over."

Her face lit up, and she smiled engagingly, "I don't know how to thank you, sir."

"Perhaps you will not wish to do so when you see the house. I must warn you that it will be in disorder. And then there is also the strange manner of Stuart's death."

She stared at him, "I beg your pardon?"

"Stuart was found by his housekeeper, Mrs. Mulliken, lying on the library floor in a pool of blood. I don't wish to shock you, my dear, but there is still some question as to how he died, although the coroner's verdict was accidental death. It's generally believed that he'd had a bit much to drink, fell and hit his head on the fireplace fender. However, Mrs. Mulliken swears the brandy decanter had barely been touched, and even Lord Eversleigh seems to suspect foul play."

Hester sank back in her chair, her smile faltering.

The solicitor reached across and patted her hand. "This must be distressing for you. Still, I couldn't allow you to go and live there without making you aware of all the circumstances. There have been other unpleasant incidents in the neighbourhood recently, too. Only last fall, Lord Mansfield, the uncle of the present one, was held up by highwaymen in broad daylight and killed. He was shot down in cold blood. Most unsettling. Then, on the day of your cousin's funeral, Silverdale was broken into and the library ransacked. As far as can be determined, nothing was taken, but it does give one pause. The Mullikens are still in residence, of course, but I own I'd feel much better if you had someone to accompany you."

Hester silently thought she'd feel better, too. Aloud, she said, "I haven't any other relations, as you know, but I've been thinking that perhaps my old governess, Miss Beckles, would be willing to come to me."

"That would relieve me. However, there is one other alternative. One which I would strongly suggest you consider. Lord Eversleigh has empowered me to settle all Stuart's debts and offer you twelve thousand pounds for Silverdale outright. You could manage quite nicely on that. I consider it a most generous offer."

"Very generous! But why is Lord Eversleigh so anxious to acquire the estate?"

"I believe it distresses him to have Silverdale in the midst of his lands, especially as young Martingale let it fall into such a disreputable state. You'll understand if you do go there."

"It's certainly an offer to be considered," she replied, visions of a tidy fortune before her. "Is there a time limit? Do I have to make a decision at once?"

"Oh, no. Lord Eversleigh has been extremely considerate. He only asked that I put the matter before you."

"Then I think I should like to see the property before deciding. Will you give me the directions?"

Rundle readily agreed, and then called in his clerk, Crimshaw. He instructed him to withdraw fifty pounds from the safe for Miss Martingale. Hester at once protested the sum was too extravagant, but subsided when Rundle reminded her that she would need to engage a post-chaise, and would have to spend at least one night on the road. Although she had intended to continue her journey on the stage, the luxury of travelling in a post-chaise tempted her too much, and she gracefully yielded.

The solicitor recommended an inn where she could put up for the night and promised he would see to arrangements for a chaise first thing in the morning. Hester was ready to set off for Silverdale at once, but reluctantly conceded the hour was too advanced. She decided to treat herself to a night at the inn, a tasty dinner, and perhaps even a fire in her bedchamber. Spirits restored, she thanked Mr. Rundle for his kindness.

The solicitor arranged for her to be conveyed to a modest establishment that would not cavil overly much at her travelling alone. Although at eight-and-twenty, Hester did not consider that she needed a maid to lend her respectability, she knew many places would nevertheless turn her away. The room she was shown to was not one of the best bedchambers, but it was large and pleasant, and the four-poster that stood in its centre looked comfortable and inviting. Hester nodded with approval, taking note of the handsome cherrywood desk beneath the windows, already stocked with stationery.

Mrs. Limbury, the proprietress, was fussing about, drawing the heavy draperies over the windows facing the courtyard. "I hope you'll be comfortable here, miss. I can't offer you a private parlour, we're that full up, but I'll have Alice bring up tea, and later a dinner tray, if that would be agreeable?"

Hester said it would, thanked her, and watched contentedly as the boy lit the fire that was laid before he shyly withdrew. She looked round the cozy room, and did a little two-step before removing her hat. What a change from Mrs. Thadge-Morton's! There she had slept on a hard and unyielding cot, and had taken her dinner with the children in the nursery. Not even on the coldest nights had her employer allowed her a fire in her room. She couldn't find it in herself to be at all sorry that she had given in her notice.

After changing her travelling dress, Hester seated herself before the desk and filled two pages with fine script explaining her new circumstances to her old governess. Becky, as she had always called her, would be both surprised and pleased by her good fortune. Hester only hoped her old friend would be free to visit with her for a month or two.

With that chore finished, she settled before the fire and enjoyed the tea the maid had provided, and thought about her unknown cousin. Stuart Martingale did not seem to have been the sort of person one would gladly claim as a relative. At least, she thought merrily, he had had the grace to die young and rescue her from the drudgery of being a governess. And even if the house was in the shambles that Mr. Rundle prophesied, there was still the tempting offer from Lord Eversleigh. With twelve thousand pounds she could buy a little cottage for herself and Becky.

The offer was certainly tempting. Still, she mused, if her cousin had been so opposed to selling the house to Eversleigh, she owed it to Stuart to have a look at it and consider alternatives before deciding to sell. The name Silverdale had a pleasant ring to it, and perhaps the house might not be as bleak as Mr. Rundle predicted. It had been a long time since she had had a place to call her own home, and Hester found the prospect pleasing.

Overly tired from her journey, she fell asleep before the fire, lost in a reverie of pleasant dreams, until the maid tapped on the door. The girl entered, bearing a lavish dinner tray, and Hester realized she was ravenously hungry. She was more than a little amused that Alice seemed in awe of her, and she greeted the girl kindly to set her at ease.

Alice dropped an awkward curtsy, apologizing profusely for being late with her dinner. Her eyes fell on the brown travelling dress laid over the chair. "If you'll let me have that, miss, I'll fresh it up for you."

"That's very kind of you, and I'd certainly appreciate it, but I fear there's not enough time. I must be ready to leave first thing in the morning. I'm travelling to Yorkshire then."

"Yorkshire! Why, that's where I'm from, and missin' it sorely, I am!"

"You don't care for London, then?" Hester asked politely, as she sampled the cornish hen.

"No miss, but I needed work, and London was the only place I could find it. Mrs. Limbury's been right good to me, she has. Still, I've been hankering to get back to the country."

"Is your family in Yorkshire, then?"

"Lud bless you miss, but I haven't any kin. I'm an orphan, you see. Raised at the County Orphanage, and taught how to be a proper maid. Mrs. Limbury says I do well enough, too."

"I'm sure you do, Alice. Tell me, have you ever heard of a place called Silverdale?"

Alice wrinkled her brow in concentration and reluctantly shook her head. "Can't say as I have, but I've been away going on four years now."

"It's situated in a village called Lower Newbury, and near Lord Eversleigh's country seat."

Alice brightened, pleased to have some knowledge for the kind lady. "I reckon as how everyone in Yorkshire has heard of Lord Eversleigh. A fine gentleman, he is. I seen him once. He came to inspect the orphanage, and me and Clarissa peeped over the banister at him. Ever so handsome he was."

Hester smiled at her dreamy expression. "Well, as he's to be my neighbour, I expect I shall meet him before long."

It was clear she'd risen another notch in the girl's esteem. Alice, suddenly struck shy, busied herself about the room while Hester concentrated on her dinner. It wasn't until she put another question to her that Hester noted the girl's wet eyes. "Alice, I apologize if I said anything to upset you. Is there something I can do?"

"Wasn't nothin' you said, miss." The girl sniffed, wiping her eyes with the corner of her apron. "It's only that

I've been so powerful homesick and hearing you talk about Yorkshire brought it all back to me.''

Hester's heart went out to the gangling maid, and she wished there were something she could do for her. An idea occurred, and she hesitantly suggested, "I've just been thinking that I shall be needing a maid. I can't afford to pay much, but you'd get room and board—"

"Oh, miss! Do you truly mean it?"

"Yes, of course, but I must warn you that the house I'm going to will probably not be in very good order. I don't really know what I'll find. And I'm afraid I can't offer you permanent employment. It may be only for a month or two."

"If I could go back to Yorkshire for just a month, I'd die happy!''

Hester laughed and extended her hand. "Shall we consider it a bargain, then? Can you be ready to travel in the morning?''

"Can I? I'll be ready at dawn, and I'll have all your things ready, too, Miss Martingale.'' Alice stumbled a little over her name, so Hester kindly suggested she simply be addressed as "Miss Hester," and then added, "What about Mrs. Limbury? Will she be distressed if you leave without notice?''

"To say the truth, miss, she'll be mightily relieved. Mrs. Limbury don't rightly need me, but she took me on as a favour to Mrs. Harrowbridge, her that runs the orphanage. I'll just go and tell her now.'' Alice scurried to the door, but popped back in again a minute later. "My head's in the clouds, I'm that excited. I clean forgot your dress.'' She disappeared again, carefully holding Hester's cloak and dress over her arm.

Hester learned early the next morning that Alice had been correct in her assessment of Mrs. Limbury's reaction. The landlady came up to speak with her, to be sure, she explained, that Alice had not been day-dreaming. "She's a good girl, and a hard worker, but terrible home-sick she's been. It's a blessing from Providence, you turning up and needing a maid to go to Yorkshire. I'm that pleased for her." She sniffed audibly, and added, "I told Alice there'll always be a place here for her, so if it doesn't work out, you just send her back to me."

Mrs. Limbury saw them off, struggling to overcome her emotion. She gave Alice a warm hug and bade her be a good girl. To Hester, she gave a heavy wicker basket, packed with just a few things, so she said, to tide them over until they reached the Posting House where they'd spend the night. She was still calling out instructions and warnings as their carriage rolled out of the courtyard.

By the time Hester and Alice approached Lower New-bury the following afternoon, they were on excellent terms, although Alice had trouble understanding Hester's sadness at having no family.

"By and large," the girl told Hester, "families are more trouble than they're worth, if you was to ask me. To my way of thinking, a family is just a burden to drag a person down. You was probably lucky you never knew this cousin of yours, but didn't your pa ever mention him?"

"Stuart's father, Cyrus Martingale, was my own pa-pa's younger brother. He left England when he was only a boy and travelled to India to seek his fortune. My own parents died while he was out of the country, and my mother's older sister took me to live with her. Mr. Run-dle told me that when he returned to England, he tried to find Papa, but it was only shortly before my uncle died that he even knew I existed. Mr. Rundle said he was anx-ious to see me, but they weren't able to find me in time. I was living with my aunt Horatia, and we rarely saw anyone. Then, after Cyrus died, my cousin Stuart wasn't interested in finding me. I'm afraid, from what Mr. Rundle said, that my cousin wasn't a very pleasant person, in any case."

"There, and didn't I just tell you? If your cousin had lived, you'd have found yourself saddled with a set of dirty dishes, mark my words."

"Oh, Alice, not all families are like that. Some are loving and loyal. They can be a real comfort."

"Hmmph! Did you ever know any that was? I seen a lot come into the inn, and not many as what got on. Most seemed to spend their time wrangling or trying to get the better of each other."

Hester was reluctant to admit that the sort of family she dreamed of was known to her only through her books, and a dim memory of a happier time when her parents were alive. She allowed the subject to drop as they entered the village of Lower Newbury. Their driver had directions to Silverdale, and seemed to know his way about. He whisked them through the tiny village before they were able to catch more than a glimpse of the shops lining the narrow street.

Her first sight of Silverdale was encouraging. The avenue leading to the house was not very long, and as soon as one rounded the bend, a view of the brick house with its imposing columns appeared. The afternoon sun flattered it, giving the bricks a soft, warm glow. A tiny duck pond was south of the house, and a small park surrounded it. Hester looked about eagerly. If one didn't notice how overgrown the park was, the first view of the house was fairly attractive.

Their chaise came to a stop in the centre of the circular drive, and Hester sat still, staring at her new home. It was both larger and better kept than she had been led to believe.

She allowed the driver to assist her down, and then bade him and Alice wait while she approached the veranda running the length of the house. Mr. Rundle had provided her with keys, but she knew the Mullikens were still in residence. She stood, undecided. Should she let herself in, or lift the heavy knocker? The decision was taken out of her hands when the door opened briefly to reveal a diminutive tow-headed girl standing beside a dog of tremendous proportions. The child took one look at Hester and the waiting chaise and slammed the door shut. Hester, torn between indignity and amusement, decided to be amused. She lifted the knocker, and the door was opened a few minutes later by an elderly woman of ample girth. She looked rather harassed, with strands of wispy grey hair escaping from her cap, and her apron sporting liberal doses of flour. Hester noted the large rolling pin held menacingly in one hand, and hastily introduced herself.

The housekeeper turned red with embarrassment, and dropped a speedy curtsy before calling her husband, Ben, to come and assist Miss Martingale. Hester was shown to the front salon, amid apologies from Mrs. Mulliken for her rudeness, and explanations that her arrival was completely unexpected. Hester paid scant attention. She'd seen the elfin child again, this time peeping curiously around the door. Hester pretended not to notice, and focused her attention on Mrs. Mulliken.

"I quite understand I wasn't expected," Hester reassured her. "But if you could just provide us with some tea and see that two rooms are readied, we shall make do."

The housekeeper showed a dour face and Hester thought that she meant to argue. Alice's entrance seemed to deter her, however, and she set off, if reluctantly, for the kitchen with Alice trotting after her. Left alone, Hester removed one of the Holland covers from a comfortable-looking wing chair near the fireplace. She happened to glance up at the large, gilded mirror over the mantel, and caught a glimpse of the little girl just edging past the door. She dropped the cover and hurried to the hall, calling out a quick hello as the child wrestled with the heavy lock on the front door. The huge dog stood protectively beside her, emitting a low growl as Hester approached.

The girl turned and hung her head, one tiny hand restraining the intimidating black dog. After a moment, large blue eyes turned upwards to study Hester. Apparently deciding the lady meant no harm, she advanced with simple dignity, holding out her hand. "Good afternoon, miss. I'm Jennifer Eversleigh, and this is Blackie."

Hester shook the tiny hand, and introduced herself. She looked a trifle apprehensively at the dog. "He's frightfully big, isn't he? What kind of dog is he?"

"Blackie's a mastiff," the child answered with just a touch of scorn for anyone who wouldn't know that. "I guess he belongs to you now. He used to be Stuart's, but I visited him a lot because he likes me. He'll like you, too, if you speak nicely to him."

Hester decided she must have been referring to the dog and not to her deceased cousin. She had doubts as to the dog's affability, but dutifully extended her hand for him to sniff, and then scratched him just behind the ear. Blackie approved. As she withdrew her hand, he rubbed his huge head against her, almost knocking her over.

Jennifer giggled. "You see, he likes you already. He's really a very good dog."

"To be sure. Well, Miss Jennifer, Mrs. Mulliken has gone to prepare tea. Would you care to be my first guest?"

Jennifer considered this, indecision plain in her eyes. One factor seemed to weigh above all others, and prompted her to respond, "Thank you. Mrs. Mulliken makes the *best* cakes." She followed Hester back to the salon, and seated herself politely on the one uncovered chair. With a smile, Hester removed another cover and sat opposite her.

"Now, tell me, are you allowed to visit here all by yourself?"

"I wasn't really visiting. Look—Blackie *does* like you." The mastiff had settled his bulk on the floor, close to Hester's chair. Jennifer continued with the candour of an eight-year-old. "I came here with my brothers to look for Stuart's treasure."

"Treasure! My, that sounds exciting! What kind of treasure?"

A shout from the doorway prevented Jennifer from answering. Hester turned to see two young boys staring disgustedly at the girl. A family resemblance was obvious, and Hester assumed they must be her brothers. Jennifer invited them to come and meet Miss Martingale. "She's going to live here, so we shall have to tell her about the treasure."

The boys came in, and the taller of the pair introduced himself. "I'm Harry Eversleigh, and this is my brother, Jack. Jenny is our sister. I hope she hasn't been bothering you, miss."

"No, indeed. In fact, she's agreed to have tea with me. Would you boys like to join us? Your sister tells me that Mrs. Mulliken makes excellent cakes."

Harry grinned. "She does! Much better than our cook. But we shouldn't stay. Our brother may be looking for us."

"Goodness, another brother? How many are there of you?"

Harry laughed at her surprise, but obligingly counted his family members off on his fingers. "Well, Charlie's the oldest, he's thirty, and he's our guardian, too. Then comes Richard, he's sixteen. I'm next, and almost fifteen. Jack here is ten, and Jenny is the baby. She's only eight."

"I am *not* a baby!"

"Certainly not," Hester intervened. "And if you will help me to remove some more covers, we can all be seated and enjoy our tea."

The covers were soon piled in a corner, and when Mrs. Mulliken returned, she found the Eversleigh children seated around Miss Martingale. Seeing her frown, Hester assured her that the children were her guests, and invited for tea. "They tell me your cakes are the best in the county."

"Well, it ain't for me to say so," she replied, obviously pleased, "but I did take the blue ribbon at the fair. I'll just go get some more of these for the children, for you won't believe how they can eat."

When Mrs. Mulliken had gone, Hester handed a cup of tea to Harry and commanded, "Now, please tell me more about this treasure."

Both boys started to talk at once, but a cuff on the arm convinced Jack to be still and let his brother speak. "We heard Charlie talking to the Justice one day, and he said something in this house must be worth a fortune!"

"Did he? How strange. I thought my cousin Stuart was deep in debt."

"That's just it," Harry pointed out eagerly. "Until last year, Stuart didn't have a feather to fly with. Then, all of a sudden, he's flush. He pays some of his debts, buys some swell horses and even some new clothes. And—" he lowered his voice "—no one knows where he was getting the money from."

"I see your point," Hester said, nodding. "Still, what makes you think it was some sort of treasure? Stuart might have had a horse come in at Newmarket, or a run of luck at cards."

"At first, that's what everyone believed. But it was the same every month. At the end of the month, Stuart was always in funds. It's no secret, 'cause that's when he had the tradesmen come round to be paid. Charlie says maybe someone was paying him to keep his mouth shut."

"You don't mean...blackmail?" Hester asked in shocked tones, willing to play along with their game.

"Well, Charlie says—"

"Charlie says you talk a great deal too much," a deep voice commented from the hall. There were cries of "Charlie" from the children as a tall gentleman entered behind Mrs. Mulliken. Jennifer ran forward to meet him, and tugging him insistently by his hand, she announced proudly to Hester, "This is my oldest and best brother, Charlie."

Lord Eversleigh acknowledged the informal introduction with a slight smile and a nod. Hester tried to conceal her dismay as she realized Lord Eversleigh was the same gentleman she had seen leaving the solicitor's office. Why hadn't Mr. Rundle told her that Eversleigh had just left?

CHAPTER TWO

HESTER WAS THANKFUL for the diversion Mrs. Mulliken created, bringing in a tray of cakes and tarts. She was able to recover a little of her composure while the housekeeper greeted his lordship fondly. There was no doubt he was popular, for even Blackie left Hester's side to fawn against Eversleigh's boots. Fickle dog.

Returning to her own chair, Hester indicated that Lord Eversleigh should also be seated.

"I hadn't meant to stay," he replied, with a hungry look at the tea tray, "but Mrs. Mulliken makes the best tarts this side of London."

"So I've been hearing. Do, please, join us. Your brothers were just telling me that you think my cousin was indulging in a touch of blackmail." She spoke mockingly, on the defensive against the handsome Charlie.

He raised a brow in surprise and looked at Harry. "Don't you think it would have been polite to let Miss Martingale settle in before you began maligning her family?"

Harry reddened. "I didn't mean...you're nothing like your cousin! I mean—"

"Enough halfling," Eversleigh interrupted. "I apologize on behalf of my family, Miss Martingale. Are you planning on making a lengthy visit?"

"I haven't decided as yet, but I shall be here for at least a month or two. The house appears to be in better condition than I was led to believe."

"Stuart's solicitor told me he had located you, but not that you intended to visit here. I was astonished when Mrs. Mulliken told me you were here."

"I fancy Mr. Rundle was also surprised by my decision. He urged me, quite strongly, to sell Silverdale outright. But I felt I owed it to Stuart's memory to have a look round the place before selling it off."

"You *can't* sell it," Jack protested. "Not before we've had a chance to find the treasure."

Hester smiled wryly. "I shouldn't worry, Jack. The offer to buy Silverdale came from your brother."

Harry looked amazed. "Charlie! What a complete hand you are. That's a capital idea, and you never told us."

"Then we can search all we want," Jack added his approval, one idea still held firmly in mind.

"Hold on, fellows. Miss Martingale has not decided yet if she wishes to sell. And I thought I told you I didn't want to hear any more nonsense about Stuart's treasure."

Neither of the boys looked very chastened by his stern tone. Harry grinned. "But you didn't say we couldn't look for it!"

Jennifer had been sitting quietly in her chair, looking back and forth between her brother and Miss Martingale. Sadly, she asked Charlie, "Don't you like Miss Martingale? *I* do, and I don't want her to sell the house and go away. Blackie likes her, too."

Hester rewarded her with another cake. "Thank you, Jennifer. I like you, too. And I promise I shall be here for a little while, at least. I hope you will come and visit me often."

"Us too?" Harry asked hopefully.

Hester laughed. "Certainly, but you may find yourself put to work. I mean to set the house in some sort of order."

"That's all right," Harry assured her. "If we help clean the rooms, we'll be able to search at the same time. I think there's probably a hidden room or secret panel somewhere!"

"Harry, that's enough! Now come along, all of you. I think we've bothered Miss Martingale enough for one day." Lord Eversleigh rose, and his younger brothers followed suit. Jennifer moved to Hester's side, and politely held out her hand. "It was very nice to meet you. Please take good care of Blackie."

"I shall, but I think he'll be lonely without you. Will you come and see him tomorrow? Say, after lunch?"

Jennifer nodded shyly, and after giving Blackie a parting hug, slipped from the room. Lord Eversleigh hung back for a moment. "I should like to discuss your cousin's estate with you, Miss Martingale, when we can be private. There are some things I feel you should know if you intend to live here."

"Like blackmail?" She smiled, finding the idea absurd.

"It's no joking matter, I assure you. May I call in the morning?"

"Very well, if you believe it's really necessary."

She saw them to the door. He seemed to get on well with his brothers and sister, and she wondered what the rest of the family was like. Alice joined her in the salon as she was gathering up the tea things, and insisted on doing that task herself. "Now, you just sit down here and put your feet up. A long day you've had, and visitors right off."

"Yes, Lord Eversleigh and his younger brothers and sister. Did you see him, Alice?"

"Indeed I did. I was readying your bedchamber, what overlooks the drive, and saw him out the window. Handsome as ever, he is."

"I'm certain a number of ladies find him so," Hester replied, her voice indicating she was not one of them.

"Don't you like him, Miss Hester?" Alice asked, considerably startled.

"It's not a question of likes or dislikes, Alice. I barely spoke with him, and I'm not at all sure that I trust him. He seems very anxious to buy this house. And, he's been hinting that my cousin was not all that he should have been."

"Humph. Mrs. Mulliken has been telling me about your Mr. Stuart. He wasn't no favourite of hers, I can tell you. She told me she only stayed here out of respect for Mr. Cyrus." Alice patted Blackie on the head as he stood patiently by the tea table, his tongue lolling out. "Good doggie, here you are," she told him as he gratefully gulped down one of the cakes. "I'm glad we have him in the house, miss. Mrs. Mulliken told me how someone broke in here the day of the funeral and ransacked the library. As far as she could tell, nothing was took, but a rare mess they made!"

Hester sat up. "Oh, dear, that sounds as if someone else believes in Harry's theory. And I thought it was all nonsense!"

"And who might Harry be?"

"Harry Eversleigh. He and Jack are the younger brothers. They were here when we arrived—searching for Stuart's hidden treasure!"

"Treasure?" Alice looked puzzled. "I thought this cousin of yours was on the ropes?"

Hester obligingly explained Harry's theory, and Alice's eyes grew large as she avidly listened. Hester concluded, "I hope you won't let this frighten you, Alice."

"No, miss. But I must say I never looked for this much excitement! Why, wouldn't it be thrilling if we were to discover something?" she asked, looking about speculatively.

"I'm glad to see you're not too frightened," Hester replied dryly. "Do you know if Blackie was in the house when it was broken into?"

"No, he weren't, and a shame that was. Mrs. Mulliken says he's a right good watch-dog. But that day he was out for a run, no one expecting thieves to be about in broad daylight!" Alice retired with the emptied tea tray, and Hester busied herself folding the linens.

Mrs. Mulliken came in shortly, full of apology because there was so little in the larder to make a decent dinner, her tone implying that if she had been given proper notice, such would not have been the case.

Hester assured her that after eating so many of the delicious cakes and tarts, she had little appetite for dinner, and a light repast would do very well. Tomorrow, she promised, Ben could drive into the village and replenish their supplies with whatever Mrs. Mulliken thought necessary. She took several pound notes from her pocket and entrusted them to the housekeeper. Mrs. Mulliken unbent a little under this uncritical handling, and responded willingly enough when Hester asked her to tell her what she could about the Martingales.

She had nothing but good to say of Cyrus, and lamented his passing still. As for Stuart, there was little she could say to his credit. She placed a great deal of emphasis on the unfortunate death of his mother in childbirth. Cyrus wasn't interested in much after his lady's passing, not even his infant son. "If you was to ask me, I think Mr. Cyrus blamed the boy for her death. Mr. Stuart looked a great deal like his mama, and it seemed like Mr. Cyrus couldn't bear to have him around. It's little wonder the boy grew up troubled."

"Well, at least he didn't let the house go completely. It's in much better order than I had anticipated, though I expect credit for that is due to you. I had thought to find it completely run down and threadbare!"

"Then you should have visited a year back. I feared for a time, the way Mr. Stuart was selling off everything, that we wouldn't have a chair left to sit on."

Hester looked round the comfortable room. There was certainly no indication here that the master of the house had been in straitened circumstances. "Of course," she told the housekeeper, "I haven't seen the rest of the house, but this room is nicely furnished."

Mrs. Mulliken beamed. "I've tried to keep it up, but with just Ben and me, it's been hard to do it all. Mr. Stuart bought those chairs just a couple of months back, and the draperies are new, too."

"I see. Mr. Rundle, Stuart's solicitor, told me that my cousin had come into some money quite unexpectedly. Did Stuart ever give you any indication of where the money came from?"

"No, miss, and so I told Lord Eversleigh when he asked me. All I know is that it was a regular thing. Someone paid Mr. Stuart a tidy sum at the end of every month. Why, he even started paying Ben and me our wages regular. Mr. Stuart was right generous when the dibs was in tune. Ben asked him once, joshing like, if he'd discovered a gold mine or something. Mr. Stuart, he just grinned. More like a golden goose, he says. Or maybe a pigeon. Ben didn't know what to make of it. Said he'd never seen Mr. Stuart in such high spirits.''

The housekeeper's words stayed with Hester throughout the afternoon and early evening. After she retired to her room, she sat for some time, gazing into the fire. If there was a mystery attached to her cousin's death, then she was going to have to unravel it, or she'd never know any peace of mind at Silverdale. Hester continued to sit before the fire, considering what she might do. As a start, she decided she would read through all of Stuart's journals and papers that she could find. With this in mind, she lit a candle.

"Come, Blackie. Let's see if we can find the library." The big mastiff looked content lying on the rug before the fireplace, but as she opened the door he lumbered to his feet and followed her. Hester had done little more than glance through the rooms earlier and thought she recalled the library was off the long hall, towards the rear of the house. She moved quietly, not wishing to disturb the others, and pushed open the wide-panelled door leading into the library. Her candle held high, she glanced nervously about the room. It was full of shadows and the furniture, still draped in dust covers, gave it an eerie aspect. She was glad to have Blackie beside her and patted him on the head.

What had seemed an excellent idea while she was seated cozily in her room, now appeared palpably foolish. Hester moved to the cabinet behind the desk and held the candle closer. There were several agricultural journals, a number of volumes dealing with thoroughbred horses and a few random novels. A cabinet beneath the shelves was found to be locked, and she moved on to the next section. She almost missed the diary. It was sandwiched between a volume of Shakespeare's plays and a book of

Byron's poems. She withdrew the slim book and riffled its pages. Most were blank, but a few were covered with a sprawling handwriting she guessed to be her cousin's. She slipped the book into the pocket of her wrapper and turned to go, when she was startled by a noise outside. Blackie, growling softly, moved towards the window. Hester whispered for him to come back, but he was up on his hind legs, front paws on the window seat. The dog gave a loud bark and growled again, pushing his nose between the heavy draperies. He barked several more times and Hester thought she heard movement in the shrubbery outside. She held her breath, afraid to move, her heart beating rapidly.

Suddenly, the door to the library was flung open, and in the candlelight, Hester saw the gleam of a pistol levelled at her. She froze for a moment before she realized the intruder was Ben Mulliken. His gruff voice demanded to know what was going on, and Blackie bounded to his side, whining to be let out.

"Ben! Thank heavens it's you!"

"Is that you, Miss Martingale? I beg your pardon, but I thought as how you had retired, and I heard Blackie barking. Thought we had another house-breaker!"

"I think we might have, if it hadn't been for Blackie. I came down to get something to read, and Blackie heard someone outside and set up the alarm. Do you think perhaps we should turn him loose?"

"Wouldn't do no harm, but it's doubtful that it'd do any good, either. If someone was there, they be long gone by now. More like, it was a stray cat."

Blackie had returned to the window, still alert but quiet. Hester decided to keep him in, and give him the run of the house in case an intruder did return. She apologized for disturbing Ben and retired to her bedchamber. Blackie padded along behind her, and she carefully left the door of her room ajar so that he might come and go as he pleased. But the mastiff seemed content to settle down once more before the fire.

"So you like a fire, too, do you?" Hester asked him, as she added more coals. They caught and flared nicely. She drew her chair closer and took out the diary. The flyleaf confirmed that the diary was her cousin's. She turned to the first entry, which was dated almost two years earlier. It was a rambling account of a successful week spent at Newmarket, where, apparently, Stuart had enjoyed a run of luck. He had begun by betting on a horse called Crow's Flight, an omen, he was sure, since a flock of crows had risen in flight as he rounded a bend in the road, nearly causing his horses to bolt. The horse had won, as had several others Stuart had backed that week. Her cousin wrote agreeably of the week he had spent with Lord Ormond while at Newmarket, and Hester dutifully made a note of the name. She did not really believe that it was likely to have any bearing on the mystery, but one never knew.

The next few entries all dealt with various wagers Stuart had staked, all of which he had won. Hester wondered idly if all the blank pages in between denoted losses. If so, her cousin had been decidedly unlucky. She discovered he was also not very particular about what he wagered on. The diary recorded bets not only on cock fights and horse races, but boxing matches, stagecoach runs, the fall of the first snow and even the outcome of the suit of a Mr. Crayon who aspired to the hand of a Miss Darcy.

She continued to make note of the various names she encountered until a huge yawn stayed her hand. She realized the candle had burnt low and judged the hour to be quite late. Blackie flicked open an eye as she moved

about, preparing for bed. She gave him a comforting pat
as she wished him a good-night and climbed between the
chilly sheets. After her earlier scare, and being alone in a
strange house, she feared a restless night. But it was only
minutes after her eyes closed, that her breathing softened
and she fell into a sound sleep.

HESTER WAS STILL SLEEPING soundly when Alice came in
the next morning and drew open the draperies. Sunlight
flooded the room, and Hester opened sleepy eyes. It took
her a minute or two to recall her surroundings, and she
only half listened as Alice chattered cheerfully.

"A perfect sort of day to be setting the house in order.
The windows can be thrown open and fresh air let in. It's
days like this that I been missing so bad! You don't get
sunny, warm days like this in London, not with a sky so
blue it fair makes a person want to sing."

Hester, smiling at her maid's enthusiasm, sipped her
chocolate. She watched contentedly while Alice tidied the
room, and noticed Blackie had deserted her. Alice explained that Ben had taken him out early for a look
round. "He told us you heard a noise outside last night.
Ben thinks it was just a cat or a rabbit, but Mrs. Mulliken insisted he take Blackie and have a look. What was
you doing in the library so late, miss?"

"Just looking for something to read, Alice. Please tell
Mrs. Mulliken that I shall be down shortly, and we can
form a plan for the day."

When Hester descended to the morning room, she
found Ben there, waiting for a word with her. Blackie
bounded up to greet his new mistress, and she had to request him quite sternly to sit. "Yes, Ben, what is it?"

"I thought you should know, miss, that I took Blackie
out, and we searched round the house. And, well, there's

a couple of shrubs beneath the library window that have been trampled.''

Hester digested the news calmly, seating herself and pouring out a cup of tea. "Then you think there *was* an intruder on the grounds last night?"

"Without a doubt, miss! There's a set of footprints, a man's boots looks like, as clear as day."

Hester carefully set her cup down. She didn't feel she could give a credible imitation of serenity if it were seen that her hands were shaking. "I think the first thing we should do is to make sure the house is secure. Would you please check all the windows and doors?" At his nod, she continued, "Blackie will be allowed to roam the house at night, and I trust he will alert us to any unusual activity."

Ben agreed to this, but was reluctant to make his planned trip to the village, leaving three women alone in the house. Hester tried to reassure him, and herself, that no one was likely to attempt to break in during the day. Alice backed her up, declaring herself ready to defend Miss Hester with her life, should it be necessary. The gleam in her eye seemed to indicate she hoped it would be. Hester, thinking to curb her maid's bloodthirsty tendencies, set her to cleaning the bedchambers. Alice went about her task with good will, and when Hester went up to see how she fared, she found the maid struggling with a trundle bed in the hall.

Alice explained she felt it was her duty to sleep in Miss Hester's room as long as there was any danger to her mistress. Telling her she was overly cautious, Hester was about to order her to put the bed back in the attic when Mrs. Mulliken called hurriedly to her. Lord Eversleigh, she said, was in the library waiting to see her.

Hester pushed a couple of errant curls beneath her mob cap, and brushed some of the dust from the front of her morning dress. She had forgot that Eversleigh was to call, and hurried downstairs. When she entered the library, he was standing with his back to her, examining some of the books in the glass case behind the desk. Blackie was nearby, and his demeanour plainly said there was nothing to fear from his lordship. Hester was not so certain. She made her presence known and invited Lord Eversleigh to be seated.

He greeted her pleasantly enough, but his quick appraisal made her wish she hadn't worn such a deplorable gown. Her morning dress was an old grey muslin which she only wore when engaged in house-cleaning or gardening. Putting the thought aside, she politely enquired of Eversleigh if he'd care for a cup of tea.

"No, thank you. I met Ben outside and he told me you had a bit of excitement here last evening."

Hester merely nodded, sure that it was unnecessary to elaborate. No doubt Ben had confided in him all the details.

He continued, "This only confirms my belief that your cousin was involved in some sort of unsavoury affair. I think you should reconsider your decision to remain here."

"I appreciate your concern, Lord Eversleigh," she answered coolly.

"But have no intention of following my advice?" He smiled as he put the question. "Come down off your high ropes, Miss Martingale."

"I fail to see what concern it is of yours, sir, whether I stay or go. However, as you are so patently interested, I will tell you that I do intend to remain here, and further, I shall do my best to discover whatever I can about Stuart's affairs."

"I rather thought that would be your reaction. I only hope you won't have cause to regret your decision. Early last year, it looked as though your cousin was rolled up. His creditors were dunning him relentlessly, and he'd sold off everything but the house and the few acres it stands on. Rundle informed me that he even put that on the market. One seldom saw Stuart when he wasn't in his cups. He neglected everything—the house, the stables, even his dress. And Stuart used to be quite fastidious in his attire." He paused, considering her reaction. Hester sat primly, and if she felt any revulsion or fright, it was not apparent.

"I think it was in March," he went on, "that he suddenly came into a bit of luck. Stuart was not a cautious man. He'd wager on the sun rising, if you dared him. Unfortunately, he was not very prosperous at either the table or the turf, and I had little expectation of his luck holding. It's no secret that I wanted to buy Silverdale. You can see how it's situated, and to have this eyesore in the middle of my lands is . . . an annoyance. Even so, I hope you will believe I did not wish Stuart any ill. If he had recouped his fortune and repaired the estate, I should have been content—although, I confess, considerably surprised."

Hester found his manner frank and engaging, but she recalled her father once remarking that the most untrustworthy scoundrels were the most charming of fellows. "I hold you excused from wishing my cousin ill. Pray continue."

"As I said, I would have been surprised if Stuart's luck had held. And so I was. Month after month, he prospered. He was not drinking so much, and he began to make improvements in the house. Even some of his creditors were satisfied. The odd thing, Miss Martingale, is that your cousin seldom left the estate. That, coupled with some strange remarks he let fall, aroused my suspicions. I take leave to tell you that Stuart was not a modest man. Had he been enjoying an extended run of luck, he would have boasted of it across the county. Then, several months ago, he was set on by highwaymen. Stuart was obviously prepared for just such an encounter and scared them off with a couple of shots. He bragged he'd wounded one of the ruffians, but Ben told me privately that he was talking of hiring a bodyguard.''

"You seem to be in Ben's confidence, Lord Eversleigh. Isn't that rather unusual, considering his master's animosity towards you?"

He laughed. "Acquit me of bribing his servant! Ben has known me since I was a lad, and Stuart, too. Ben knows I wouldn't do anything to harm Stuart, whatever your cousin may have thought. And Ben was concerned over Stuart. He knew something was afoot. When Stuart died, we feared matters had come to a head. While it's generally believed that Stuart fell, ostensibly under the influence, Ben swears he was sober that day."

"How could Ben say so, one way or the other? I understood that he and Mrs. Mulliken had gone to Harrogate to visit their daughter and didn't return until late that evening."

Eversleigh nodded. "That's true. But Ben said Stuart had been drinking very little and was sober as a judge when they left. Stuart was expecting a caller that day, and Mrs. Mulliken had set out the brandy decanter. She swears it was hardly touched. She was the one to find him, when they returned, in this room."

Hester couldn't help glancing at the fireplace. Her lively imagination pictured her cousin stretched out on the floor, his head split open. Eversleigh's words brought her attention back to him.

"He was lying, just there, with Blackie beside him."

"But, surely if Blackie was here..."

"You're thinking Blackie wouldn't have let a stranger in. I agree. However, anyone who knows the dog would have nothing to fear. I will say only that I found Stuart's death somewhat suspicious. It wasn't until the house was broken into on the day of his funeral that I became convinced your cousin really was blackmailing someone, and the proof is somewhere in this house."

"Then you don't believe that whoever broke in, and searched the place, found what they were looking for?"

"I wondered, of course, but your intruder last night leads me to think otherwise."

Hester rose. "I appreciate your confiding in me, but it still does not alter my decision. If my cousin somehow stumbled upon something...something so terrible that he could extort payment for his silence, then it is a matter that should be brought to light."

Lord Eversleigh stood beside her. "Your attitude may be admirable, Miss Martingale, but it is also extremely foolish. Whatever knowledge Stuart possessed very likely cost him his life."

"I understand that, sir. You've made it quite clear."

"Have I also made it clear, Miss Martingale, that if you persist in remaining here, against my advice, your own life may be in danger?"

CHAPTER THREE

LORD EVERSLEIGH'S abrupt departure left Hester shaken, and unsure if his parting words had constituted a warning or a threat. She didn't see him for several days, but Harry, Jack and Jennifer kept her apprised of his opinions on every subject. She was growing fond of the younger Eversleighs, and their liveliness made Silverdale seem a great deal cheerier. It was only their constant habit of beginning every other sentence with "Charlie says" or "Charlie thinks" that grated on her nerves.

That he was first oars with his siblings spoke volumes for his tact and diplomacy, but Hester was still of the opinion that he was too puffed up with his own consequence. She told Alice it would do him good to have *someone* disagree with him on occasion.

Alice held it was difficult to disagree with a gentleman as nice in his tastes as was his lordship, and one who had such uncommon good sense besides. Since both of the Mullikens seldom lost an opportunity to praise Lord Eversleigh, Hester began to wonder if she were the only person to find his air of unquestionable authority unpalatable.

She did give him credit for taking such good care of his brothers and sisters, but reasoned that was because he was so much older than they. Mrs. Mulliken had told her that Lady Eversleigh had suffered a number of stillbirths between Charles and the birth of Richard. By the time the younger ones were born, Charles Eversleigh was old enough to be looked up to, but not so old as to be excluded from their confidence. The result was that all the younger children adored him.

She was still ruminating on the dire consequences of allowing a young man undisputed rule of a large household, when Jennifer visited her. She found Hester upstairs busily sorting linens and setting aside those in need of darning. Judging from the growing pile of tablecloths, sheets and pillow cases, she would have ample needlework to occupy her for some time. Jennifer seated herself on a footstool, her head in hands, and watched Hester as she worked.

"You're very quiet today, Jenny. Is something wrong?"

"Our new governess is coming tomorrow, and I won't be able to visit you very often. She'll make us do lessons every day," Jenny replied darkly.

Hester laid down the tablecloth she held, and sat in the chair beside the child. Her hand caressing the blond curls, she told her, "But all children have to learn their lessons. You wouldn't want to grow up not knowing anything, would you?"

"I wouldn't care!"

Hester smiled. "But what would happen when you got married and had your own home to run? Besides, your new governess may be quite nice, and you'll enjoy your lessons."

"That's what Charlie says. But I won't. I want to come here and see you and Blackie and help the boys look for treasure."

"Well, the boys will have to study, too. And you can still visit sometimes. I'm only sorry that you are getting your governess before I get mine."

Jenny looked at her, large brown eyes measuring Hester to see if she were teasing. "You're too old to have a governess," she scoffed.

Hester laughed. "Indeed I am. But when I was your age I had a governess whom I called Becky. And, you know, I liked her so well that I have asked her to come and live with me. She should be here any day."

This was clearly a new idea to be considered. Governesses, in Jennifer's opinion, were cranky old ladies who were forever criticizing one, and making one do lessons when the sun was shining brightly out of doors. That anyone could be so fond of a governess as to ask her to live with her voluntarily was unheard of.

Hester continued, "I'll tell you a secret, too. Before I came to live here, *I* was a governess."

Jennifer studied her suspiciously. "You don't look like a governess."

"Thank you. I take that as a high compliment, but I promise you, I was. Only my charges were so bad that I ran away!"

"I wouldn't be bad if *you* were my governess. But I didn't like Mrs. Alverston, and neither did Harry and Jack. Charlie says she was a very good lady, and we should be ashamed of putting frogs in her bed."

"So I should think! What did Mrs. Alvertson do?"

Jenny smiled at an obviously pleasant memory. "She screamed so loudly that she woke everyone up! And she wouldn't sleep in her room anymore, so she had to spend the night in the blue room. She talked to Charlie for the longest time the next day. I don't know what she said because they were in the library with the door shut. Then Charlie made us apologize to her, and he sent her back to Town in his own carriage. Charlie was a little angry with us, and said we must never do such a thing again. But if we don't like Miss Fontaine, we shall think of something else to do to make her go away! We've had four governesses already," she told Hester proudly.

Hester could almost feel a little sorry for Charlie, and she began to think her own tenure as a governess had not been so terrible. She did what she could for Miss Fontaine. "I wouldn't do anything, if I were you. Your brother will only engage another governess."

"Why can't *you* come and be our governess?"

"What? And have you put frogs in my bed? No, I thank you."

Jennifer giggled, and with her spirits restored went off to find Blackie.

Hester returned to her linens, her mind on poor Miss Fontaine. But a few minutes later, a shout from Harry drew her into the hall. He was halfway up the stairs, and called excitedly for her to come quickly and see what they had found. She followed him down, through the formal dining room and into the breakfast room.

Jack was just emerging from a cupboard, imperfectly concealed in the wall to the left of the fireplace. Cobwebs hung in his hair, and a wide streak of dirt blackened his cheek. His eyes were aglow with excitement, and he made it clear that he considered Hester to be the most fortunate person alive.

Jennifer, standing outside the cupboard holding a candle, nearly set the room aflame as she jumped up and down, demanding to know if he'd found the treasure. A loud thump from within the cupboard gave Hester a start, but it was only Blackie following Jack out. He, too, bore evidence of the disreputable state of the cupboard.

"I don't mean to depress your spirits," she told them, "but this is only an old wardrobe cupboard, and it's not even set in very neatly. I don't think Stuart would have chosen such an obvious place to hide anything."

"*We* know that," Harry assured her loftily, as he urged her forward. "But do you know what's *in* it?"

"Cobwebs and dirt, obviously. One has only to look at you. And I will *not* set a foot in there!"

Harry accepted what he regarded as her undue concern with a little dust and merely begged her to have a look. Hester took the candle from Jenny and held it up as Harry nimbly jumped in. He was on his knees in a flash, and Hester watched, amazed. What had appeared to be a solid wood floor was now pried up into two sections, revealing the beginning of a flight of stone steps.

"Good heavens!" Hester said faintly. "Come out of there at once!"

Harry looked at her in surprise. "Don't you want to see where it goes? I waited for you before I explored it, because it's yours, after all. So that was only fair. Shall I go first?"

"No, you shall not! And neither will I. Whatever would I say to your brother if you fell and broke your leg?"

Jack and Jenny laughed, and Harry reassured her. "Much Charlie would care. I promise you, he's quite used to us breaking bones, and he never makes a fuss." He disappeared from view, and Jack scrambled in after him. Hester grabbed him by his collar.

"Wait right there. One of you in that hole is enough. Jenny, watch what you're about—I almost set your hair on fire." The three of them peered over the edge of the cupboard and Blackie whined to be let in, too. The candle provided little light, and only the first three steps were visible.

"By Jove! Miss Hester, you won't believe this!" Harry's voice floated up to them. "There's a neat little room here, with a cot and a chair and another door. Wait a bit."

"Harry, come back up. That's enough until we get more light." Hester called down to him, her voice seeming to echo within the cupboard. There was no answer, and she waited a few seconds before calling again. There was still no answer. She began to feel uneasy, supposing him to have fallen. Visions of him lying down there, unconscious or worse, floated before her. Jennifer and Jack shouted to him, but only a weak echo of their voices answered them.

Jack looked at her, alarm beginning to show in his eyes. "Should I go after him and see what's happened?"

"No. I'll go. And if I don't call back up to you right away, you run and get Ben. Understand?" He nodded, and she was about to climb over the edge of the cupboard when Harry strolled into the room behind them.

"Only fancy, the door down there leads right into the gardens!" he said by way of greeting.

"Harry! You abominable, odious boy. What a fright you gave me!" Hester scolded him, but he was apparently accustomed to this form of address and simply grinned at her.

"It's not too dirty in that room, Miss Hester. If we were to take some candles, we could go in through the gardens and have a good look round." He wiped a cobweb from his shoulder and added, "It's mostly the steps that are full of spiders."

Hester shuddered. The younger Eversleighs were anxious to explore the room hidden below, sure that the treasure must be stashed there. She knew a strong impulse to bolt the cupboard securely shut and forget the existence of that room. Only the realisation that the door outside would have to be secured as well made her yield to their entreaties. They gathered up as many candles as they could carry, and Harry led the way out to the gardens.

Hester and Alice had walked through the gardens several times. Beyond noting that they were wildly overrun with weeds, and had obviously been neglected for years, neither had paid much attention to the yard. Hester felt a little better as she breathed in the fresh air. She looked around hesitantly, but there was no sign of another entrance into the house, save for the kitchen door.

"You wouldn't guess there was any other way in, just looking, would you? Clever, I call it," Harry said, grinning.

Jack scampered to the stone wall that formed the north side of the house and peered into the shrubbery covering it.

"Not even warm," Harry called to him.

"Harry, if you don't show us where that door is immediately, I shall—"

"Gad, Miss Hester, I didn't mean to tease you. I thought you'd *like* to look for it first." He led the way to the corner of the house where a trumpet vine had taken over and covered the wall with its creepers. Pulling these aside, Harry stood next to a door clearly revealed in the sunlight. Hester watched apprehensively as he pulled it open. Jennifer, slipping her hand into Hester's, stood staring with large eyes. Harry and Jack ran ahead eagerly and lit several of the candles. Hester lifted her skirts and she and Jennifer slowly followed.

With the candles lit, the room looked less menacing. There wasn't much to be seen. An old cot stood to one side, a cane chair standing near it. The steps leading up to the breakfast room began in the centre of the small cell. The other wall was lined with shelves, but these were bare except for an old book and a half-burnt candle. Apparently the room had only been used as a temporary shelter, or perhaps a priest's hole.

Hester's keen eyes noted that there was very little dust on either the cot or the chair, but she didn't mention that to the children—or that the door hadn't creaked when it was opened. A simple latch locked the room from inside, and she discovered it was rusted through. A hard shove from outside would snap it in a minute. She determined to have Ben secure the room as soon as she returned to the house. The thought that anyone could have entered while they slept left her feeling decidedly queasy. She patted Blackie on the head, thankful for his presence in the house.

There didn't seem to be anything potentially harmful in the room, and she told the boys they might continue to search, while she went to find Ben. There were loud protests when she revealed her intention of shutting the room up.

"Yes, I know it's very cowardly of me. Only think how exciting it might be to have a thief steal into the house while I'm asleep."

"Well, if you're worried about being murdered in your bed, you need not. Blackie would protect you," Harry reassured her, and Jack added his representations that Blackie was the best watch-dog in the whole country.

She did not voice her opinion that the mastiff was also the most undiscriminating of creatures in his quests for food. The dog would eat anything, and she could too easily imagine an intruder tossing him a chunk of poisoned meat. She left them to their search and set out to find Ben.

Hester found him in the still-room, verifying their store of supplies. At first, he was disbelieving. She finally succeeded in convincing him that there was indeed a hidden room and stairway. He seemed as pleased as the boys and readily agreed to come at once, supposedly to secure the door. Hester suspected he was as eager as Jack to explore the room.

They were halfway down the corridor when a dreadful scream rent the air. Hester lifted her skirts and ran the rest of the way to the breakfast room. Harry was calling for her in an agitated manner, and she could hear Jenny crying. With total disregard for spiders and cobwebs, she climbed into the cupboard. Ben, loudly voicing his astonishment, was right behind her.

"Harry, are you hurt? What was that scream?"

"Oh, do come quick, miss. It's Jack. He fell down the steps, and he won't wake up."

Hester carefully descended the narrow steps as rapidly as she could. At the bottom, she saw Jack stretched out on the floor, his head cradled in Harry's lap. Jenny was sitting by him, wiping tears from her eyes and imploring Jack to wake up.

Hester's heart gave an uncomfortable lurch as she looked at the still form and Jack's unnaturally pale face. She knelt beside him and quickly ascertained that he still had a pulse, although it was very faint. One of his arms seemed to be bent at an awkward angle, and she feared it was broken.

"Harry, is there a doctor nearby?" At his nod, she commanded him briskly, "You must go for him at once. Take the grey, and ride as fast as you can. Tell the doctor what happened and that Jack is unconscious. Ask him to come right away."

He nodded again, his own face ashen, and slid his brother's head into her lap. He stood up to leave, then hesitated. "He won't die, will he?"

"No, not unless it's from a beating your brother will likely give him. He's broken an arm, and I think he's just unconscious from the pain. Now hurry." She hoped her words sounded convincing.

Between them, Hester and Ben carried the boy to a guest chamber and laid him tenderly on the bed. He looked so tiny and forlorn lying in the centre of the large four-poster that Hester resolutely blinked back a tear.

"Jenny, would you go and find Mrs. Mulliken and ask her to come to us?" The little girl slipped quietly from the room, and Hester turned to Ben with worried eyes. "You don't think it's more than a broken arm, do you, Ben?"

"If he comes round, I shouldn't fret. It's his being out that bothers me." Even as he spoke, Jack opened his eyes and let out a small moan.

Hester sat down gingerly on the edge of the bed and gently soothed the blond curls back from his forehead. "Lie still," she told him, "you've had a nasty fall."

"My arm hurts awfully," he murmured before closing his eyes again.

Mrs. Mulliken came bustling in, declaring she didn't know what the world was coming to, what with secret rooms and hidden stairs. She made sounds of disapproval as she examined Jack but didn't seem overly alarmed.

She told Hester the boys had been breaking bones since they were babes, before asking her assistance in getting Jack undressed and into bed. The boy was fully conscious now, but he didn't protest as she cut his shirt and jacket away. She ordered Ben to fetch one of his own night-shirts, and then wrapped that voluminous garment about Jack's shoulders. He bore it all stoically, only once letting out a groan as his arm was moved.

When they had him settled as comfortably as possible against the pillows, Mrs. Mulliken left him in Hester's care. She would, she declared, make him a good, nourishing broth.

Hester sat down beside him again and took his good hand in hers. "Harry's ridden for the doctor, and he should be here very soon. I'm sure he'll give you something to ease the pain."

Jack tried to smile, though it was only a shadow of his usual grin. He was very pale, and Hester couldn't help wishing the doctor would arrive. Jenny solemnly approached the bed, and Hester placed a comforting arm around her shoulders. Jack looked at her and, in a low whisper, said, "Tell Charlie I won't be home for dinner."

Jenny dutifully smiled and then looked up at Hester. "Mrs. Mulliken says Jack will have to stay here all night."

"Yes, I should think it would be pretty rough on your brother to try to move him now."

Jenny considered this for a minute, and then confided, "I wish I had broken *my* arm."

Hester hugged her impulsively. "Please don't think that's necessary to spend the night here. If I'm not totally in your brother's black book, I'll ask him if you can't stay and bear Jack company."

A knock on the door heralded Harry's arrival, and he stepped in with a short, heavy-set gentleman, who was wearing the conventional frock coat and wig of a man of medicine. He cast an eye at his patient before introducing himself to Hester as Dr. Layton.

"I've heard quite a bit about you, Miss Martingale. Now don't fret yourself over this imp. This isn't the first time he's broken a bone, and I'm equally sure it won't be the last. Now then, Master Jack, what devilment have you been up to?'' Jack managed a sickly grin, and braced himself against the doctor's prodding fingers.

When Dr. Layton finished, he motioned to Hester to follow him from the room. Outside the door, he told her, ''I've given him something to kill the pain, and it will put him to sleep for a while. His arm is broken, right enough, and I'm afraid I'll have to reset it. Perhaps you could take Jenny and Harry out with you and send Mrs. Mulliken to me. She's helped me dozens of times, and she'll know just what to do.''

Hester agreed, and quietly asked him please to see her when he was done. She motioned for the children to join her, and made for the drawing room, intending to send for tea. Alice was there before her and had everything arranged. Hester accepted a cup from her thankfully and sank into the chair cushions, allowing the children to help themselves. Jenny sat next to her, as was her custom, but Harry continued to pace about the room. He could see that Miss Hester looked exhausted, and he held himself responsible.

''I'm sorry I let Jack do such a hare-brained thing as breaking his arm, miss, but he'll be fine. Why, he's taken dozens of falls before this. And Charlie will only say that it serves him right for scampering about like a monkey.''

''Oh, Lord!'' Hester cried, half rising, ''I forgot about your brother. Harry, you must ride home at once and inform Lord Eversleigh of what has happened!''

''Oh, I don't have to ride, Miss Hester. It's just a short stroll if you go through the woods. The thing is, we're late now, and either Charlie or Richard will come looking for us. If I were to walk, and Charlie brings the gig by the drive, I'd miss him completely.''

Hester eyed him with exasperation, but she was too tired to argue with his logic. In any case, she was forestalled as Mrs. Mulliken showed Dr. Layton in. Hester rose to greet him and, barely controlling her anxiety, invited him to stay for tea. When the doctor was settled with tea and a slice of Mrs. Mulliken's cake, she asked about Jack.

"He's sleeping now, and will for some hours. I reset the arm and fashioned a sling for him, not that I delude myself thinking he'll use it. However, he's young and healthy, and the arm should knit without any problems, though I confess I'm a little concerned over the injury to his head. Took a nasty fall, poor boy, and a fair-sized knot to show for it. Now don't you go fretting, but I'd just as soon he stay where he is for a few days."

"I certainly have no objection to that, although I can't speak for Lord Eversleigh. One could not blame him if he feels I've been extremely negligent in caring for Jack!"

"Ha! Not Eversleigh," said the doctor with a laugh. "He's grown too used to the boys' escapades to be unsettled by a broken arm." He turned to Harry and asked, "How's that leg of yours doing, young man?"

"Capital, sir. It's as good as new." To Hester, he explained he'd broken his leg last spring, when he'd tried to jump from the stable roof to his horse's back. Unfortunately, Cloud, his mare, had bolted.

"Good Lord! I pray you won't try anything like that here."

"No, miss." He grinned. "Charlie made me promise not to do it again. Still, I think I could have made it if Cloud hadn't been so nervous."

The doctor grunted, and helped himself to another piece of cake. "See what I mean? Well, as I was saying, I'd like Jack to stay in bed for a few days. I'll be back in the morning to see how he does."

He was about to take his leave when Lord Eversleigh, having been admitted by Ben, strolled into the room. They all began to talk at once until Eversleigh held a hand up. "Enough! Ben has told me what happened. How is Jack faring?"

Dr. Layton told him, explaining that he wished Jack to remain at Silverdale for a few days. "A blow to the head can do strange things to a body, and while it doesn't appear to have hurt that hard skull of Jack's, there's no sense in taking unnecessary risks."

Eversleigh nodded and gestured to Hester. "It appears I'm to be obliged to you for a few days. Shall I send over my valet to assist you?"

"Oh, no. We shall manage perfectly well. Mrs. Mulliken is to nurse him. And, indeed, I must beg your forgiveness for allowing Jack to hurt himself. Please do not speak of obligation."

A tiny hand tugged at her gown, and Hester, remembering her promise, added, "And if you should not dislike it, Jennifer could stay and bear Jack company. I promise you, I should take good care of her."

Charles Eversleigh smiled, and when he did in just that way, it lighted up his eyes, and made one wish to smile back. "I've no doubt of that, Miss Martingale. Jenny sings your praises night and day. I must admit I grow excessively tired of forever hearing what *Miss Hester* says!"

His words brought a blush to Hester's cheeks, and a large smile to Jenny's face. Harry felt himself ill used and protested that if Jack and Jenny were to stay, he should remain as well, to look after them.

His older brother ruffled his hair. "Yes, an excellent job you did looking after Jack today!" Harry had the grace to redden, and tried to explain how the accident had occurred. But at the first mention of the hidden stairs, Eversleigh stopped him.

"What's this? Ben only told me that Jack had fallen down a flight of steps."

"Charlie, it's the *best* thing! Only imagine, Miss Hester has a secret room right in the house. We don't have anything half as grand at the manor!" Eversleigh smiled over the boy's head at Hester, and she gave him a full explanation.

"And if you wish to see that *horrid* room and steps, I'm sure Harry will show it to you."

Harry could barely contain his impatience as his elders saw Dr. Layton out. He had, most generously, offered to show the doctor their secret room, but Dr. Layton pleaded another call waiting, not to mention Mrs. Layton and his dinner.

Reminded of dinner and the lateness of the hour, Hester detained Lord Eversleigh. "If you wouldn't object to potluck, I should be pleased to have you and Harry remain for dinner."

Harry was in favour of staying, exclaiming that Mrs. Mulliken's potluck was twice as good as the fancy French food they got at the manor. His lordship, however, declined. "It would mean leaving Richard alone to consume a dinner intended for five. I fear my chef would be offended beyond words. Harry may stay, however, and if you will have me tomorrow, instead, I shall be delighted to accept."

That settled, Harry led the way to the breakfast room, and his brother remarked that he seemed quite at home. "I hope he hasn't been making a nuisance of himself." Harry objected to this obvious injustice, and Hester came to his defence. She told Eversleigh, quite honestly, that she was pleased to have his company, and that of Jack and Jenny, as well.

As they entered the breakfast room, Harry went straight to the cupboard and opened it. Hester handed a candle to Eversleigh, and he watched intently as Harry demonstrated the trick floor.

"And these steps lead to a room downstairs? If you would not object, Miss Martingale, I should like to have a look at that."

Hester did not see what harm it could do, and suggested that Harry take him in through the garden door— if Ben hadn't already secured it, which she doubted. She excused herself from joining them, intending to look in on both Jack and dinner. Jenny elected to go with her brothers and followed them out.

Hester, once assured that Jack was sleeping peacefully, and that Mrs. Mulliken had dinner well in hand, stole upstairs to change her dress. Alice, who seemed to be learning to anticipate her wishes, was waiting for her.

"Oh, miss! That Lord Eversleigh should call and catch you looking such a fright!"

Hester, amused, glanced in the cheval glass and owned that her maid had not overstated the matter. Her hair was in disarray, and part of a cobweb was clinging to one curl. Smudges of dirt decorated her face, and she noted the hem of her gown was badly soiled and one pocket torn half off. Hester silently gave Lord Eversleigh credit for his address; not by a blink of an eyelid had he betrayed any surprise at her appearance. Slightly dismayed, she recalled the first time she had met him, when she'd been travel stained and dusty from the long drive. On their second encounter, she'd been wearing an old housedress that she normally reserved for cleaning.

She allowed Alice to brush her hair into order and, after washing her face and changing her gown, hurried back to the drawing room. Harry and Jenny were waiting for her.

"Charlie asked me to convey his regrets," Harry said. "He had to hurry home before Richard raised the alarm. He said he'll send Richard over in the morning with some clothes and such. And Mrs. Mulliken says dinner is ready as soon as you might be."

"Well, let's not keep dinner waiting," Hester replied, vaguely disappointed.

Jenny had been watching her, and as she took her hand, she pronounced, "You look pretty. Harry, did you know Miss Hester was a governess once?"

"Go on. Don't try to gammon me!"

Hester had to laugh at his stricken expression. "I assure you that I was. Not all governesses are cranky old ladies, you know."

They passed a pleasant dinner as Hester regaled them with some of her former students' exploits. Harry was easily able to top these, and confided some of their more outrageous pranks. The unfortunate Mrs. Alverston rose a notch in her esteem. She had withstood a number of the Eversleighs' tricks before succumbing to flight at the appearance of frogs in her bed.

Hester tried not to laugh, and she felt she owed it to governesses everywhere to deplore Harry's behaviour. She did her best, calling him a reprehensible boy, but he only grinned, and she told him, "I'm surprised your brother hasn't engaged a tutor for you and Richard, since you take such shameless advantage of a governess."

"Well, he did consider it once, but Richard is happy studying with the Reverend Mr. Nolte at the rectory, and I'm not at all bookish."

"No! I never would have guessed such a thing. And is Richard *bookish*?"

"Lord, yes! He studies Latin and mathematics, and I don't know what all besides. What's more, he likes it! Richard wants to sit for the examinations at Oxford, and the Reverend Mr. Nolte is helping him."

"I see. And what of you, Harry? I gather Oxford doesn't figure in your future?"

"Not by half! It's the cavalry for me, if Charlie will only allow it. He's our guardian, you know."

Harry would have talked on for hours about his passion for a regiment, but Hester noticed Jenny was having difficulty keeping her eyes open. She sent Harry off to assist Ben in securing the house and took Jenny up to her own room.

Alice had succeeded in setting up a trundle bed in Hester's room, and suggested to Hester that the child might like to sleep there. When appealed to, the little girl nodded shyly. Hester helped her into an old nightdress that was several sizes too large. Jenny, padding barefoot across the floor, looked very sweet in it, with the sleeves rolled up and the hem trailing. She climbed into the trundle bed and snuggled under the covers. It was very cozy in the room, with the fire going and Blackie lying peacefully in front of the hearth. Hester thought she'd read a little more of Stuart's diary, and sat down in the chair near the fire. She'd read only a few pages when Jenny called out to her.

Laying the diary aside, Hester went to the trundle bed and looked down at Jenny. "Yes, dear, what is it?"

"Would you kiss me good-night, Miss Hester?"

"Of course. I'd love to." Suiting action to words, Hester leaned over. Jenny's arms came up about her neck, holding her close for a moment. When she lay back down, Hester pulled the covers up round her and watched as Jenny closed her eyes. As she turned away, she heard Jenny say softly, ''You smell just like my mother did.''

CHAPTER FOUR

THE NIGHT PASSED uneventfully, and Hester rose early the next morning. She donned a soft blue muslin day-dress left over from her London début. She had discovered that when all the decorative frills and laces were removed, the dress became a simple but elegant garment which was vastly more becoming to her short stature. Her only ornament was a deep blue satin ribbon threaded through her dusky curls. Feeling that she looked her best, Hester left Jenny sleeping and quietly descended to the morning room.

She stopped just short of the doorway, startled by the sight of a strange youth seated at her breakfast table. He had not heard her approach and did not look up at her entrance, so engrossed was he in the book propped open before him. Hester had ample time to observe him unnoticed. She decided he must be Richard Eversleigh, for he appeared to be about sixteen. Hester coughed to make her presence known, and the lad looked up. It took him a few seconds to recall his surroundings, and then he jumped up, almost overturning his cup of chocolate.

Hester greeted him calmly. "Good morning. I'm Miss Martingale, and you, I think, must be Richard Eversleigh. Pray be seated." She took the chair opposite and poured out her own tea as Richard begged her pardon for making free of her hospitality. He explained how Mrs.

Mulliken had insisted that he have some hot chocolate while he waited for her.

Hester cut short his rambling apology, remarking, "I'm very glad she made you comfortable. Have you come to see how Jack does?"

"Yes, miss. And I brought clothes for him, and Jenny and Harry, as well. Though I'm surprised that Charlie allowed them to stay after they put you to so much trouble," he told her, censure in his tone.

Hester raised her brows to mock surprise. "Do not tell me you doubt your brother's wisdom, or you shall disillusion me. I thought everyone believed Lord Eversleigh to be omniscient."

Richard couldn't help smiling. "I know what you mean, and the worst of it is that, in general, Charlie *is* always right! But he's never odious about it, and doesn't throw it up to you."

Hester didn't trust herself to answer this and turned the conversation by enquiring what subjects he was studying. Harry's rather noisy entrance disrupted their discourse. Jenny followed behind him and came at once to Hester's side. It was obvious that both children were quite at home in her house, and Richard viewed with patent disapproval the lack of ceremony with which Harry greeted his hostess. He was also tactless enough to chide his younger brother for his carelessness in allowing Jack to be injured.

Harry fired up at once. "If Charlie don't hold me to blame, there's no reason for you to do so!"

Richard eyed him sadly. "You mistake my meaning. I blame only myself. I should have come with you yesterday."

"Well, it wouldn't have done any good—you know Jack will never mind you. Besides—" Harry grinned

"—he considers a broken arm well worth the adventure we had, and we did find a secret room!"

Richard was more interested in this, and it was soon arranged that after Harry dressed, he would show him their discovery. Hester reflected that they might as well set up a ticket booth and charge admission for tours. She spoke only in jest, and then had to restrain Harry, who enthusiastically endorsed the idea.

She kept Jenny with her, and after the little girl had finished her breakfast and dressed, they went down to see what had become of the boys. Jenny suggested they take the short route through the breakfast room, but Hester held out for the garden entrance. When they emerged into the bright courtyard, Blackie galloped up, greeting them with loud barks that brought Harry to the door. Richard had, for once, forgot his books, and it was only with Hester's appearance that he remembered he was due at the rectory, and bid her a hasty goodbye.

Harry dejectedly reported that their search had not turned up anything new, and there did not seem to be many hiding places in the barren room. Hester and Jenny watched for a few minutes as he continued to test the wall for loose stones. Looking idly about her, Hester suddenly realized that the book she'd seen on the shelf was now missing.

"Harry, did you remove the book that was in here, or did Ben?"

"No, miss, but Charlie did. He took it with him last night. He said it was just an old farming journal, and he wanted to look through it. I told him you wouldn't object, Miss Hester. You don't, do you?"

"No, I don't suppose it was of any importance," she said, although she couldn't help wondering why Eversleigh hadn't mentioned it. Recollecting that he had left without waiting to see her again, she wondered if that had anything to do with the journal and decided to ask him about it at dinner.

She left Harry to his search and took Jenny along with her to visit Jack. They found him trying to persuade Mrs. Mulliken to allow him out of bed. He instantly appealed to Hester for support. But she, too, refused until Dr. Layton gave his permission. Jack looked mutinous, and Hester feared he would be out of bed the moment he was left alone.

It went against her principles to bribe a child, but she nevertheless offered to bring him Stuart's diary if he'd stay in bed and study it for clues. "I do think there must be some hint in it, don't you? And if you are very clever, perhaps you shall find it and solve the mystery."

Jack readily agreed to the scheme and admitted quite modestly that he *was* very clever. She brought him the diary, and also paper and pen so that he might jot down all the names he came across. Jack had decided that most probably Stuart had left a clue in code. "Isn't it fortunate that I broke my left arm, Miss Hester? Else I shouldn't be able to write."

While unable to agree that anything about his accident could be termed fortunate, Hester wisely refrained from saying so. She left him fairly content and with a bell at hand in case he needed to summon Mrs. Mulliken or herself.

The housekeeper agreed to look in on him from time to time, and Hester, finding herself reasonably free, had decided that she and Jenny might visit the village, when she heard Ben's voice and some sort of commotion going on in the front hall.

With one accord, she and Jenny went out into the upstairs hall to see what was happening. One glance over the banister was all she needed, before she gathered up her skirts and flew down the stairs, calling out, "Oh, Becky! I'm so glad to see you!"

Hester was instantly enfolded in the comforting arms of her old governess and patted encouragingly on the back. She stepped back for a better look at Miss Beckles. Becky had always been slender, but now she appeared gaunt. New lines had been etched in her face, and Hester thought she looked overly tired. Impulsively, she kissed the leathery cheek and then turned to introduce her. It was only then that she noticed the gentleman standing just inside the doorway.

The gentleman, whom Ben announced as Lord Mansfield, was a difficult man to overlook. He was so wide of girth that Hester wondered how he had fit through the door. He bowed slightly and Hester was certain she heard a corset creak. A person who appeared to be his valet stood just behind him, a creature as thin as his master was stout. He had small black eyes and a manner which bordered on the insolent and continued to stare while his master greeted her.

"Miss Martingale, I have come to pay my condolences on the loss of your cousin. A sad affair. I myself lost my uncle under similar tragic circumstances."

Hester glanced helplessly at Becky. Lord Mansfield clearly expected to be invited in, and it was clearly too late to deny herself.

Becky suggested, "Why don't you show his lordship to the drawing room, dear? Mrs. Mulliken will help me get settled, and then I'll join you."

Reluctantly, Hester obeyed, after asking Ben to show his lordship's valet, Bartholomew, to the servants' hall. Her hopes that the call would be of short duration were dashed when she observed that it took Mansfield several

minutes to ease his bulk into a chair. She very much
doubted that he could be induced to rise again for some
time. With a resigned sigh, she told him, "I must thank
you for your kindness in calling, sir, but I should explain
that I was not at all acquainted with my cousin."

"A thousand pities. A most congenial young man. I
was quite distressed to hear the news of his passing."

Hester felt an instant antipathy towards him and could
not help retorting, "Thank you. It is refreshing to hear
someone speak well of Stuart. You are the first to do so."

Mansfield tittered. "Have you been listening to idle
gossip, Miss Martingale? Ah, there are many who would
malign poor Stuart, even in his grave. Well, the boy had
his faults, I know. Still, he was kind to his friends, among
whom I was fortunate to count myself. You look surprised, Miss Martingale. I know you're thinking that I am
a good deal older than your cousin. It's true, yet he looked
upon me as a sort of father I think. He had no one else to
turn to, you know."

"I see," she said. "And did my cousin perhaps confide in you?"

"Yes, yes indeed. Quite frequently. I only wish I had
not been absent when he most truly had need of me."
Mansfield managed to extract a handkerchief from his
vest pocket and held it touchingly to his eyes.

Unmoved, Hester noted the red, bulbous nose and the
bloodshot eyes. She thought it more likely that Mansfield had been a drinking companion of Stuart's. "I hope
you will not take offence, sir, if I enquire whether Stuart
ever spoke to you of... of his finances?"

Mansfield made a show of looking puzzled for a minute, and then his brow cleared. "Aha! You are referring,
I gather, to the rumours of Stuart's sudden wealth. A very
good run of luck, Miss Martingale."

Hester returned no answer, and he continued, "It saddens me to have to tell you that there are persons who resented Stuart's good fortune. Those who had hoped to take advantage of the boy's bad luck. Yes, it's a deplorable state of affairs when a man stands to lose his home, and then recoups his fortune, only to have slurs cast on his name!"

Hester stared in disbelief. "Are you really suggesting that someone wished to acquire Silverdale enough to wish Stuart ill? For what possible reason?"

"Have you not observed how the house is situated? Why, it cuts up the surrounding land. I don't hesitate to tell you, poor Stuart's only living relative, that he confided in me, many times, how his neighbour persecuted him. Surely, Stuart's solicitor has informed you that Eversleigh has tried to buy Silverdale countless times?"

"Yes, but—"

"I would be doing a disservice to Stuart's memory if I did not warn you that Lord Eversleigh will no doubt try to force you into selling Silverdale to him. I feel I owe it to the dear boy at least to put before you a counter-offer. I know Stuart would turn in his grave should Eversleigh ever succeed in buying this house."

"*You* wish to buy the house? What on earth would you do with it?"

"As to that, I have a young nephew, a cavalry officer, who is to be married soon. It shall be my bridal gift to him."

She studied him for a minute before asking, "Did Mr. Rundle tell you the full extent of Lord Eversleigh's offer?"

"No, no. It would have been improper in him to do so. But whatever it is, I am prepared to exceed it by one thousand pounds," he announced with the air of one bestowing a munificent gift.

"Lord Eversleigh has offered to settle any outstanding claims against the estate, and give me twelve thousand pounds in addition," she told him.

"Well, upon my soul! Twelve thousand pounds!" He swallowed convulsively and used his handkerchief to mop his brow. His small eyes narrowed, and he looked at her speculatively. "I confess I'm surprised at such a generous offer. I had not expected... but that is of no matter. My offer stands, Miss Martingale."

Hester laughed, but not unkindly. "If this continues, I shall find myself a wealthy young woman. Your offer is certainly impressive, and I shall take it into consideration, Lord Mansfield. However, I am considering the possibility of residing here myself."

Mansfield looked hot and uncomfortable. Hester knew she should offer him some refreshment, but she did not do so, in the hope that he would take his leave. He appeared to be struggling to rise when Blackie bounded into the room. The large mastiff took instant exception to the stranger and placed himself before Mansfield's chair, growling menacingly. Mansfield sank back, his face turning a pasty white.

Harry, who was not far behind the dog, called him to heel at once and apologized for bursting in on them. "I didn't know you had a caller, miss, but Jack wanted to see you at once."

"Thank you. Now, please take Blackie out with you, and tell Jack I shall see him directly," Hester said curtly, fearful that Harry might blurt out something indiscreet.

When he was sure the dog was safely away, Mansfield heaved his bulk out of the chair and demanded, "Wasn't that one of Eversleigh's brood?"

"Yes, that was Harry."

"I own myself astonished to see one of that bunch so at home in Stuart's house! Your cousin would not tolerate his presence here! Why, he held the entire family in aversion and believed they were responsible for much of his misfortune."

She struggled to remain calm and managed to reply with tolerable composure, "Whatever differences Stuart may have had with Lord Eversleigh, I scarcely think a fifteen-year-old could have had anything to do with my cousin's adversity. Now, I really must excuse myself."

She saw Mansfield out, listening impatiently to several passionate pleas to consider his offer, and assuring him that she would bear in mind what Stuart would have desired. She sighed as she closed the door and turned to find Becky beside her.

"If I were not so glad to see you, Becky, I would give you a fine trimming for not coming to rescue me from that odious person."

"Was he, Hester? And he looked quite genteel! Well, I'm sorry, but I know you won't be vexed with me when I tell you Jack has made an exciting discovery! I've been vastly entertained by your young friends, and they have been telling me of your adventures here."

"What? Have you made their acquaintance already?"

"Yes, and what a delightful trio they are. Now, you must come and see what Jack has found in your cousin's diary. I declare it is just like something out of a novel."

Hester needed no further urging, and they entered Jack's room together. He looked greatly improved, and excitement had given a rosy colour to his cheeks. She noticed immediately that his arm was out of the sling and admonished him to put it back at once. He did so and then handed her the diary.

"It's an entry in the back here, and it *proves* that Stuart was blackmailing someone. *And*," he added dramatically, "that he feared for his life!"

Hester took the slim volume to the window where the light was better and read aloud the entry marked the first of January.

"His lordship must think I'm a fool. He set upon me three ruffians who halted my carriage. I have no doubt they would have killed me had I not been prepared for just such an encounter. I had my pistols by me, and I'm sure I wounded one of them. Not so brave when faced with an armed man, the three of them took to their heels. I wonder if they are the same men his lordship employed before? The one I wounded looked suspiciously familiar. The price for my silence has just doubled, and when I see his lordship on the morrow, I shall tell him so. And if he thinks to be rid of me so easily, I shall warn him that proof of his villainy is hidden within the house. He might succeed in murdering me, but I have contrived such a clever hiding place that sooner or later his foul deeds will be discovered. I know the fool will never think to look in such an obvious place..."

Here the writing trailed off, as though Stuart had fallen asleep or, as Hester thought more likely, passed out from drink.

She looked up to find four pairs of eager eyes gazing at her and felt a chill run down her spine. She was sorry she had given Jack the diary. This was no game they were playing.

Harry was the first to speak. "Don't you think that proves Stuart was blackmailing someone, Miss Hester?"

"What's an *obvious* place to hide something?" Jack wanted to know, struggling over the word.

"Well, if it's a slip of paper," Becky said, "an obvious place would be with other papers. Have you looked through your cousin's papers, Hester?"

"No, not really. Everything is sealed until Mr. Rundle comes. But I don't think Stuart would have left anything so incriminating in his personal papers. That would be the first place anyone would look."

Harry reminded her that the house had been broken into on the day of Stuart's funeral. "How do we know that this lordship didn't find whatever it is then?"

Hester would have liked to believe that the thief had found it, but the memory of the intruder Blackie had scared away convinced her otherwise. Further discussion was postponed by the arrival of Dr. Layton, wanting to examine his patient. Becky took a reluctant Harry and Jenny away with her.

Jack, who had been looking quite normal and healthy, suddenly let out a feverish groan, and his head fell back on the pillows. Hester rushed to his side, while the doctor stood eyeing the small boy suspiciously.

"What's to do, Jack? I thought you were looking very well when I came in."

Jack rolled his head from side to side and murmured faintly, "I think it's a relapse!"

Hester gazed at the doctor in astonishment. Layton winked at her and picked up the boy's arm, feeling for a pulse. "A relapse, is it? Now that's peculiar. First time I ever heard tell of a relapse from a broken arm. This could be serious, and here I thought he was well enough to go home tomorrow."

His blue eyes popped open and Jack groaned theatrically, "Oh, no! I don't think I can even get out of bed, sir."

Hester turned away to smother a smile. With her back to the patient, she asked, "Will you have to bleed him, Doctor?"

"Maybe. Hard to say. Might have to break the arm again."

Jack jerked his arm back and winced at the pain from the sudden movement. "It's not that bad, sir. I probably just need to stay in bed for a few more days."

"Stop playing your tricks off on me, lad. You're as healthy as a horse, outside of that arm, and Nature will take care of that." He turned to Hester. "Looks as if you have made a conquest, Miss Martingale. He may not want to leave you, but Jack can be sent home tomorrow."

"Thank you, Doctor. However, I suspect it has less to do with my charm and more to do with the arrival of a new governess."

"Ah, I think I begin to see. No wonder he had a setback." Dr. Layton refused her offer of refreshment and left, chuckling to himself.

Hester returned to the drawing room, still disturbed over the entry in Stuart's diary. She wondered if her cousin had made good his threat to tell "his lordship" the price for his silence had doubled. It seemed more than coincidence that the entry in his diary had been dated just shortly before his death. And had he also made good his threat to tell the mysterious lord that *proof* was hidden within the house? If he had done so, then not only was she in danger, but she had placed Becky in danger, as well. Whoever Stuart had been blackmailing must have been disconcerted to find that she had taken up residence at Silverdale.

Becky came in, searching for her, and at once scolded, "Whatever are you doing sitting here in the dark, Hester? It's enough to give one the dismals." She drew open the heavy draperies, allowing sunlight to flood the room.

Hester tried to explain her fears. "I feel terrible, Becky, asking you to come here and involving those boys in this madness."

"Nonsense!" the stalwart governess told her. "This is the most exciting thing that has ever happened to me. And I intend to stay until we get to the bottom of this!"

"Thank you, Becky, but I don't think you quite realize... Why, we might be murdered in our sleep! I suspect my cousin was murdered, and if that is true, we are dealing with someone who's terribly desperate."

"That's as may be, but only consider how foolish it was to eliminate your cousin before finding the proof he wrote about. No, I think your cousin's death came about quite by accident. And the one attempt to break into the house failed. I'm certain our villain will try other means now."

"What sort of 'means'?"

"Oh, something more devious. He'll use some pretext or other to get into the house or to get us out of it. Which reminds me, what did Lord Mansfield have to say?"

"He claims to have been a close friend of Stuart's, although there is a vast difference in their ages, and... Becky! He offered to buy the house. You don't think—no, it's too absurd!"

"Well, I should think offering to buy the house to be a very good move. Then he could search it at his leisure. Lord Mansfield should be put at the top of our list of possible candidates."

Hester smiled at the image of the corpulent Mansfield searching the house. She was sure he could not even bend over. "He'd probably instruct that sly-looking valet of his to conduct a search for him."

"Don't underestimate Mansfield, my dear. I didn't like his eyes. And, he is a *lord*."

"Becky! You said he looked quite genteel. And if we're going to consider every lord, you might as well add Lord Eversleigh's name to the list. He offered to buy Silverdale, too."

"He doesn't sound likely, in view of what the children have told me. Still, I believe it would be wise not to trust anyone until we know more. I should like to have a look at him."

"To inspect his eyes?" Hester teased, and then glanced at the mantel clock. "You shall have your chance—very shortly. He's coming to dinner tonight. Where are Harry and Jenny?"

"With Jack. Hunting for more clues, no doubt."

"Oh, Becky, I do wish I'd never given that diary to Jack. I only did so to keep him quiet. I hate involving the boys in this."

"Humph. Trying to keep those children out of it would be like trying to stop a runaway team. But there's not much harm they can do, you know."

The knocker heralded the arrival of Lord Eversleigh, and a few minutes later Mulliken ushered him in. Hester, performing the introductions, could see Becky was impressed with Eversleigh.

Eversleigh didn't comment on her improved appearance, but there was an appreciative look in his eyes. "I saw Dr. Layton earlier, and he told me Jack is fit to come home tomorrow—in spite of his relapse."

"Yes, and what a shameless poseur your brother is, sir. If you could have seen the act he put on! Why, Edmund Kean could not have done any better."

"It's all your fault, Miss Martingale. How can the manor possibly compete with a house that has a secret room and holds the key to a mystery?" He spoke in jest but was quick to note that the laughter left her eyes. "What is it? Has there been more trouble?"

"No, not trouble, precisely. But I'll admit I'm a little worried," Hester responded, and related the news of Jack's discovery. As she spoke, she began to feel that the whole affair was ridiculous. Here were Becky, placidly knitting in her chair before the fire, and Lord Eversleigh, sitting with his long legs stretched out, black boots gleaming in the firelight. Neither showed the least bit of concern.

Eversleigh did not actually smile at her, but said quite calmly, "It's not really news, you know. This only confirms my beliefs. Still, I realize it must be a little disconcerting for you to know that your cousin was involved in this sort of skulduggery."

"Disconcerting? What a talent you have for understatement, sir. To learn that the last of my relatives was an unscrupulous blackmailer and very likely murdered—"

"Come now, Miss Martingale. You never knew the fellow, so there can be no reflection on you. Even the best of families have a black sheep in their flock."

"And you, no doubt, are the Eversleighs'!"

Charles Eversleigh only laughed, but Becky remonstrated with her not to fly into a tantrum. "We shall need our wits about us if we're to solve this riddle, and I'm sure his lordship only meant to console you. Tell him about your caller, why don't you?"

Hester shot her a dark look, and Eversleigh looked to Mrs. Beckles for enlightenment.

"Lord Mansfield," the lady obliged.

"Mansfield? Now, that is interesting. Did he call to pay his condolences?" he asked, ignoring Hester's wrathful countenance.

"So he said," Hester replied shortly. Then, obeying his unspoken command, she reluctantly added, "And he offered to buy Silverdale."

"Ah, I wonder. . . what excuse did he give for wishing to acquire the property?"

"It's to be a bridal gift for his nephew."

Eversleigh grinned at her. "Do I dare ask what answer you returned?"

Hester saw an opportunity to get her own back and replied sweetly, "I promised I'd consider his offer, since he said he'd exceed your offer by a thousand pounds. Lord Mansfield also said he knew Stuart would turn in his grave if you were ever to gain possession of his home. He believes my cousin held you in aversion, and blamed you for much of his misfortune."

"Possibly. The boys were forever playing off their tricks on Stuart, and he never failed to rise to the bait. Once, last year, they stole out of the house, and while your cousin was in the village tavern, they switched his horse with a donkey. It's said Stuart didn't know the difference until he was halfway home."

"Harry and Jack did that?" Becky asked, much surprised.

"Oh, no. That time it was Harry and Richard. And I promise you, they were both restricted to the house for a month."

"Richard! I can hardly credit it," Hester said. "I thought he was the one member of your family above reproach."

"That happened last year," Eversleigh said with a laugh. "This year, Richard would not dream of doing such a thing. Thank God!"

Alice rang the dinner bell, and Hester went to round up the younger Eversleighs. Jack was allowed out of bed for the occasion, although he had some difficulty managing with one hand. Hester noticed that Lord Eversleigh kept a watchful eye on him and twice helped the boy out unobtrusively.

Dinner passed merrily, but when Mrs. Mulliken looked in for the third time, obviously wishing to clear the table, Hester suggested they adjourn to the drawing room. The boys and Jenny engaged in a riotous game of spillikins, with Becky acting as judge.

Eversleigh took advantage of their preoccupation to draw Hester aside. "You've done Jenny a world of good, and for that I'm deeply indebted to you. She's been rather withdrawn since our parents died, but lately, and especially tonight, she seems more like her old self."

"Perhaps she's only been missing feminine companionship?"

"Perhaps—except that she's never taken to any of the governesses we've had. In fact, she always seemed to resent their presence. The last one she wouldn't mind at all, and several times she ran away and hid. I've been at a loss to know what to do."

"Well, I've done what I can to help Miss Fontaine, and I hope you'll continue to let Jenny visit me, after her studies. Perhaps if she knows she may, she won't mind doing her lessons."

"I think what I should do is buy Silverdale away from you and hire you to be her governess."

"Thank you, but no. I've had enough of that. If I do sell the house, I intend to buy a tidy little cottage where

Becky and I may grow old together in comfort and peace."

"Miss Becky perhaps may do so, but I doubt there will be much peace where you are, Miss Martingale. No, don't glare at me. I meant that as a compliment. You cut up a man's tranquillity without in the least meaning to."

Hester suspected that he was roasting her, but he had turned to settle an argument between the boys, and they had no further opportunity for private conversation. Harry and Jenny pleaded to be allowed to spend one more night at Silverdale, and Eversleigh yielded to their wishes. He left with a last warning that he'd be on the doorstep very early, to collect them for their first day of lessons with Miss Fontaine.

It was not until Hester had tucked Jenny into bed and kissed her good-night that she realized she'd forgot to ask Eversleigh about the missing book from the secret room.

CHAPTER FIVE

LORD EVERSLEIGH was as good as his word. He called promptly to collect the younger Eversleighs, and the house seemed dismally silent after their departure. Hester decided to spend the morning sewing, while Becky announced her intention of tackling the attics. Hester protested, but Becky insisted she would enjoy the task.

The morning passed slowly, and it was not until after lunch that a diversion occurred. Hester had settled on the drawing room as the most comfortable place to work, and Mrs. Mulliken had thoughtfully placed a tea tray close at hand. The fire provided a pleasant warmth, and Hester felt herself growing drowsy with the monotony of the endless mending. She perked up when she heard the knocker, thinking it must be one of the Eversleighs. Mrs. Mulliken appeared after a moment, followed by a very stylishly clad and attractive young woman.

"Miss Derringham," the housekeeper announced dourly.

The lady advanced, holding forth her hand, and Hester stood amid the clutter surrounding her, to greet her. She felt clumsy and ill dressed beside the tall, willowy figure of Miss Derringham, and she did not miss the disdainful look that lady cast at her mending.

Hester invited her guest to be seated, cordially offering her tea. Miss Derringham politely declined, saying she did not mean to intrude for long. "I can see you are busy, only it is such a lovely afternoon, and Charles—that is, Lord Eversleigh—told me of your arrival. I just had to drive over and see Stuart's little cousin for myself.''

"Oh, were you acquainted with my cousin, ma'am?''

"Lord, yes! Stuart and I had a great deal in common. We both felt stifled living in this God-forsaken village. I escape whenever I can to London. Stuart, poor boy, found his escape in the bottle. Though I can almost envy him, escaping this place forever.''

"Do you find it so unbearable, then? It seems such a pretty place.''

"It's well enough in its way, I suppose, if one cares to be buried alive. My soul cries out for the theatre and balls and routs. London is so much more amusing. But you shall find out for yourself, if you stay here for long.'' Her delicate hands with their long, tapered fingers gestured as she spoke, and the rings adorning her hands sparkled in the light.

Hester studied her guest, noting the luxurious auburn curls which formed a perfect frame for the piquant face. She had lovely, almond-shaped eyes, heavily fringed, and a tiny beauty mark on one cheek. Hester could not help wondering what a lady with the sophisticated tastes of Miss Derringham was doing in Lower Newbury, but she curbed her curiosity and replied pleasantly, "I'm afraid I've been too busy trying to set my cousin's house in order to notice any lack of entertainment. And although I've been here for such a short time, I have had plenty of visitors.''

"Charles told me his younger brothers and sister have been here nearly every day. How tiresome for you.''

"Not in the least. I enjoy the children's company.''

"Really? I never could abide having children about. It's very upsetting to my nerves. But, then, I believe I heard someone say you were formerly a governess? I suppose that would account for your tolerance."

Hester smiled at the thinly veiled condescension, and wondered to what purpose Miss Derringham had called. Her visit was certainly not motivated by friendliness. She replied sweetly, "Yes, I was a governess until Stuart left me this house. Now, I'm considering settling here permanently."

"You cannot be serious! Why, my dear, there isn't a decent shop in the entire village. No theatre or balls. And the assemblies they get up are not even worth mentioning. Really, Miss Martingale, it would be most unwise. I'm certain you would regret it."

"And yet, *you* live here."

"Ah, that is a different matter. I come down solely to bear dear Lord Eversleigh company. He cherishes some silly notion that this is an ideal place in which to raise children. I do hope to convince him that his younger brothers should be away at school. The girl, too. It would do them a world of good, besides teaching them some much-needed manners."

Hester did not comment, and Miss Derringham continued, "It has been hopeless since his parents died. Charles is a devoted brother, and they take shameless advantage of him, keeping him tied to the manor."

"I gather you have known Lord Eversleigh for some time, then?"

"Oh, since we were children ourselves. There has always been a kind of understanding between us. Things would be very different if his parents had not died so inopportunely."

Hester was tempted to reply that it was very inconsiderate of them, but held her wicked tongue in check. A slight movement by the door caught her eye, and she looked up to see Jenny. She called out to her, "Come in, my dear. I'm sure you know my guest."

The little girl walked slowly in and dropped a quick curtsy to Miss Derringham before scurrying to Hester's side. She seated herself on a footstool and did not utter one word until Miss Derringham took her leave.

Miss Derringham did not seem disposed to linger after Jenny's entrance, and Hester saw her to the door. When she returned to the room, Jenny instantly demanded, "What was *she* doing here?"

"Miss Derringham came to pay me a call, and you were not very courteous to her."

"I don't *like* her!"

"That's as may be, but you must be civil to guests in my home—if you wish to continue visiting me."

"Even if I don't like them?"

"*Especially* when you don't like them. It is the mark of a true lady to be able to behave civilly to persons one dislikes."

"Why?"

Hester eyed the child with exasperation. "Because we are a civilized people, and we behave politely to others at all times. Trust me, Jenny. Generally, it makes life more pleasant for everyone."

Jenny considered this carefully before asking, "Do *you* like Miss Derringham?"

"Really, Jennifer. You shouldn't ask such a question. Besides, I don't know the lady well enough to form an opinion. Why do you dislike her so much?"

"'Cause she only pretends to like Harry and me. She wants to marry Charlie, and then she'll send us all away."

Hester was at a loss for words. She saw the fear in the child's eyes and impulsively hugged her. "Well, I think Lord Eversleigh is much too fond of you to let *anyone*

send you away. Now, tell me about your new governess.
Is she nice?''

The governess, it seemed, was nice enough, though not
anything like "Miss Hester" or "Miss Becky," who continued to rate high with the younger Eversleighs. The afternoon passed pleasantly, and it was only occasionally
that Hester reflected on the strange visit from Miss Derringham. Not until after dinner did she have an opportunity to discuss her with Becky.

They settled comfortably in the drawing room, pleased
with the day's work. Becky had some sort of book and
papers before her, and Hester asked her curiously what
she was doing.

"I retrieved your cousin's diary from Jack, and I'm
making a list of the names in it."

"I wish you luck. I started doing that before I gave it to
Jack, but most of the names only seemed to be persons he
wagered against."

"Well, now, your cousin did give us a clue of sorts. He
wrote as how it was a *lord* he was going to see. It stands
to reason that this lord is one he knows, and I've made a
list of all the ones he mentioned. There are six in all. Lord
Eversleigh and Lord Mansfield we've already met. Then
there's a Lord Wincanton, Lord Petersham, Lord White,
and..." She paused, looking at Hester solemnly before
adding, "Lord Derringham."

"Derringham? Do you think it was more than a coincidence that Miss Derringham called today? She must be
his daughter, I think."

"She is. Mrs. Mulliken told me Derringham is a wid-
ower, and fairly dotes on his only daughter. *She* has her
cap set for Lord Eversleigh and no doubt came only to get
a look at you."

"What nonsense you talk, Becky."

"Humph. She came fast enough when she learned Eversleigh dined here last night. Mrs. Mulliken says she's been trying to bring him up to scratch for years. But the children don't take to her, nor she to them."

"That I can believe. Jenny wouldn't speak a word to her. She thinks Miss Derringham wants to marry her brother and then send them all off to school."

"She would. She's a Society lady who thinks children should be neither seen nor heard. She'd turn them over to a nanny and governess or ship them off to school. I know her type well, Hester, and my heart goes out to the poor children."

"If you're worrying over our young friends, don't," Hester replied. "Eversleigh strikes me as having a rather autocratic disposition, and I doubt anyone is capable of persuading him to do anything he doesn't wish. In any case, it's no concern of ours, and we're digressing. It is Lord Derringham we should be discussing, and the other peers on your list. Lord Wincanton, did you say? I think we can cross his name off—I met him during my London Season. He absolutely loathes the country and never leaves Town. According to Stuart's notes, our villain must either visit here frequently or live in the vicinity."

"Why, I hadn't thought of that," Becky said, beaming at her. "You're right, and that means we can also eliminate Lord White. Mrs. Mulliken says she never heard of him, and she's certain he never visited Stuart. I'm sure she would know of him if he lived anywhere nearby. That leaves Lord Petersham and Lord Derringham. Petersham resides about a day's ride from here. He and your cousin were particular friends, and he often visited Silverdale. Mrs. Mulliken said they frequently went to the races together."

"And Lord Derringham also lives close by." Hester sighed. "I suppose we're making progress of a sort. Now what?"

Becky considered her question and at last replied, "I presume we shall have to wait for our lord to make the next move."

HER ANSWER left Hester uneasy. That night she slept restlessly, waking several times as the old house creaked and groaned. Even Blackie had a bad dream, and woke her, growling in his sleep. She slept late the next morning, and Alice, who was sleeping peacefully now that she was back in her beloved Yorkshire, chided her relentlessly for wasting such a beautiful morning.

Hester dressed grumpily and went down to the morning room, muttering about the disgusting habits of persons who were unbearably cheerful before breakfast. Her temper improved as she drank her tea and helped herself to several of Mrs. Mulliken's hot buttered scones.

Becky, who had been up for some time, came in from the kitchen garden for a second cup of tea. She joined Hester as she sat reading her correspondence, and enumerated several schemes for improving the garden until it was obvious that Hester's thoughts were elsewhere.

"I thought I might plant some watercress, and perhaps some cherry tarts on the side."

"That's fine, Becky."

"Hester! Whatever do you find so absorbing? You just agreed that we should plant cherry tarts!"

Hester laughed. "I'm sorry, Becky. My mind was wandering. There are two items here of interest. One is a letter from Mr. Rundle, Stuart's solicitor. He'll be here in the next day or two to begin sorting out Stuart's papers. I must ask Mrs. Mulliken to make another room ready."

"And the other?" Becky asked.

"Other? Other what?" Hester looked up, puzzled.

"Lord, child, have your wits gone begging? You said there were two things of interest. What's the other one?"

"Oh. A note from Lord Eversleigh inviting us to dinner tomorrow evening. He writes it's to be a quite informal affair, and he has invited several of our neighbours."

"Why, how thoughtful of him," Becky said, her eyes full of approval.

"Thoughtful? I wish I might think so." She looked at the note in her hand again. "He says he is certain that by this time I shall have discovered a burning desire to meet such gentlemen in the neighbourhood as Lords Petersham and Derringham. And he thinks I will enjoy renewing my acquaintance with Lord Mansfield, and hopes he may be of assistance."

"He's a knowing one. He's obviously come to the same conclusion we have, that our villain must be one of the lords in the neighbourhood. How obliging of him to arrange a meeting." Becky helped herself to another scone, her appetite whetted by her exercise in the garden.

"I wonder," Hester mused, "if he realizes that *he* is also suspect."

"He'd be a fool if he didn't, with all the hints you've thrown out," Becky told her bluntly. "And in my opinion, he's anything but a fool."

"Yes, and that worries me. He could be playing us very cleverly."

"Really, Hester, I don't know why you're so determined to make Eversleigh out the villain, but I can tell you this. It was a stupid man who let himself be ensnared by your cousin, and even you must admit that Lord Eversleigh is not stupid!"

Hester, surprised by Becky's vehement defence of Eversleigh, was moved to protest. "But Becky, it was you who told me not to trust *anyone*."

"So I did, and it's what I still say. But at least keep an open mind. I shouldn't like it if you were to let his good looks and charm beguile you into trusting him indiscriminately. On the other hand, I don't wish to see you offend him without reason."

"Well, far from offending him, my suspicions seem merely to cause him amusement."

Becky nodded, looking hungrily at a dish of fresh strawberries. "If you do decide to remain here, Hester, I hope you'll persuade Mrs. Mulliken to stay on. She has such a light hand with pastries, and the roast beef we had last night was excellent. I don't know when I've tasted better."

Hester could not judge whether Becky intended the housekeeper to hear her remarks, but Mrs. Mulliken entered in time to hear the last bit, and her pleasure was obvious. She fairly beamed at them, but only said, "Alice said as how you wished to see me, miss?"

"Yes, I've had a letter from Mr. Rundle, and he should be here in a day or two to go through Stuart's papers. Do you think we can have another room readied for him?"

"Of course, Miss Hester. The blue room at the end of the hall should do nicely, unless you wish to give him Stuart's room?"

"I suppose we shall have to deal with it sooner or later, but for the time being, I prefer to leave Stuart's room shut up. Let's put Mr. Rundle in the blue room, and after he has gone through any papers that might be in my cousin's room, we can turn it out."

"Yes, miss." She turned to leave, hesitated and turned back. "If I might say so, Miss Hester, it does my poor heart good to see the house full of people again, as it was when Mr. Cyrus was alive. And it's a pleasure to cook for folks what have an appetite to appreciate what's set before them!" She blushed at having put herself forward, and hurried from the room before Hester could reply.

"Well, this has been a morning for surprises. What next?"

Becky agreed and added, "You know, Hester, this would not be a bad place to live. The kitchen garden is not beyond repair, and we could easily grow all our own vegetables. I've made an excellent start."

"Now, don't do too much, Becky, until we know more. While I agree that it could be made into a charming home, I'm not at all sure I shall be able to afford to live here. It all depends upon what Mr. Rundle discovers."

She left Becky and made for the stables in search of Ben Mulliken. He'd be needed to drive them to Eversleigh's for the dinner party. Ben promised to set to work at once cleaning up the old carriage to make it habitable for her and Becky. Things were looking up, Hester thought. Now, if only she could find something presentable to wear. The dinner was to be informal, but she'd wager her last groat that Miss Derringham would come dressed in the first stave of fashion.

She was right. When Hester and Becky arrived at the manor the next evening, they found Miss Derringham acting as unofficial hostess. She hurried to greet them, and Hester was thankful she'd followed her instincts and worn her best. Though both Becky and Alice had assured her that she looked quite elegant, Hester considered that only kindness. She didn't notice the admiring looks several of the gentlemen present cast in her direction. She was too intent on studying Miss Derringham's attire.

The lady wore a shimmering white satin that obviously was the latest style, and looked as if it came straight from Paris. It clung so closely to her lush figure that Becky whispered she'd dampened her petticoats to get that effect. The décolletage was very low, exposing the tops of her creamy breasts, and a diamond pendant nestled between them, drawing all eyes. Diamond clusters clung to her earlobes as well, and a diamond bracelet encircled one of her slender wrists.

Hester, standing next to her, felt like the proverbial country mouse. She didn't realize the simple cut of her own green silk was vastly becoming, or that the small cameo she wore at her throat gave her a look of refreshing innocence compared to Miss Derringham's opulence.

Her hostess was all sweetness as Hester made her known to Miss Beckles, and she gushed her pleasure at seeing Hester again so soon.

Lord Eversleigh crossed the room to welcome them warmly, and Hester had time to admire his evening dress, which, she admitted, suited him perfectly. He greeted Becky first, quizzing her on the pretty flowered turban she wore, telling her she was far too young to be dressed like a dowager. He won a smile in response and a rap on the knuckles from her fan. "Don't you be trying to turn me up sweet, my lord. You save your pretty compliments for Miss Martingale, who at least deserves them."

"Yes, Charles, doesn't she look sweet," Miss Derringham drawled, taking a possessive hold on his arm.

Eversleigh directed his attention to Hester, and she felt a blush suffusing her cheeks as he looked her over critically. He finally remarked, "I don't believe 'sweet' is the adjective we want. Here, Percy, we need your opinion."

He addressed a foppish gentleman, mincing his way towards them on jewel-studded high heels. "Miss Martingale, may I make you known to Mr. Percival Mansfield?''

Percy bowed before her, his highly starched shirt points precluding his turning his head to any degree. The ruffles and ribbons he wore, and the flower in his coat, proclaimed him a tulip of the ton. Eversleigh explained to him that his unerring judgement was wanted. ''Hermione would have it that Miss Martingale looks very *sweet*. What is your opinion?''

Hermione Derringham was evidently annoyed by all the attention being shown to a mere governess. Her smile was forced as she continued to cling to Eversleigh's arm. Hester, embarrassed with the by-play, suspected they were making sport of her. She lifted her chin and held herself proudly as Percival put a quizzing glass to his eye and studied her.

''I think,'' he pronounced slowly, ''that Miss Martingale has the look of a newly opened rose, freshly kissed by the morning dew.''

Hermione tittered. ''Really, Percy, I had no idea you were so poetic.''

''But astute. I knew your judgement could not be faulted,'' Eversleigh said. ''And now, Percy, would you be so good as to amuse Hermione while I make Miss Beckles and Miss Martingale known to the rest of my guests?''. He deftly transferred Miss Derringham's hand to Percy's arm and drew Hester and Becky away.

''I believe you already know Percy's father, Lord Mansfield,'' he continued smoothly, as they approached his portly neighbour. Mansfield, who had been in conversation with a tall, heavy-set man, greeted Hester warmly, though he spoke rather condescendingly to Miss Beckles. The quiet man next to him was introduced as Lord Petersham. Both Becky and Hester eyed him with considerable interest, but there was nothing in his dress or manner to raise the slightest suspicion of villainy.

Petersham had more the look and build of a country squire than a peer of the realm. His long red hair and full beard hid much of his face, but his blue eyes seemed to twinkle beneath a pair of shaggy brows. "So you are the infamous 'Miss Hester' my lady and I have been hearing so much about from Miss Jennifer," he teased. "I hope you'll be making a long stay, for her sake."

"Thank you, my lord, but our future is undecided as yet."

"Well now, I wouldn't be wishing you away, but if you should be deciding to sell Silverdale, you must let me know. I have a spinster sister who means to set up on her own, and Silverdale would make a nice little house for her, where I could be keeping an eye on her."

"Now just a moment, Giles," Lord Mansfield interrupted, "I've already made Miss Martingale a handsome offer for Silverdale!"

"I don't know of any law that says she has to accept the first offer made, Louis," Petersham replied jovially. To Hester, he added, "If it's agreeable, I'll call by later in the week, and we can discuss it further, if you're still of a mind to sell, which I hope you won't be."

Eversleigh, who had stood silently by, a faint smile on his lips, excused himself and the ladies and took them across the room to meet Lady Petersham. She was as tiny as her lord was tall and, like him, dressed rather plainly. Her face was that of a peasant, lined and deeply tanned from exposure to the weather. She smiled at both ladies, and Hester felt instantly that here was a person she could trust.

Lady Petersham had been sitting with the Reverend Mr. Nolte, his wife, Natalie, and their daughter, Rebecca.

Eversleigh performed the introductions and allowed them a few minutes of conversation before whispering to Hester that he had promised Jenny to bring her up to say good-night.

They slipped quietly from the room, and only Miss Derringham watched with sharp eyes as Eversleigh assisted Hester up the grand staircase. He showed her to the door of Jenny's room. "I'll wait for you downstairs. Don't let Jenny keep you too long or my guests will accuse me of hiding you away."

Hester was thankful for the brief interlude, which gave her an opportunity to compose herself. When she descended the stairs, she saw Becky seated near the fire with Lady Petersham, and quietly made her way to them. Eversleigh, standing and impatiently listening to a debate between Miss Derringham and Percy Mansfield, followed her movement with his eyes. He was about to join her, but Hermione, who had also noted Hester's return, promptly turned to him with a question. Politeness demanded that he give her his attention, and she saw to it that he remained by her side until dinner was announced.

Since the gathering was to introduce Hester and Becky to their neighbours, Eversleigh treated them as honoured guests. Little though Hermione might like it, Hester was seated on his right, and Becky on his left. That Hermione was not best pleased was obvious. She paid scant attention to either Lord Mansfield or the Reverend Mr. Nolte. Every time Eversleigh addressed a remark to Hester, she sat forward, straining to hear their conversation.

Hester, who was aware of the frequent, hostile glares sent her way, tried to direct most of her conversation to Lord Petersham. They touched on his friendship with her cousin briefly, and Petersham expressed his sorrow at Stuart's unexpected passing. Petersham seemed a simple man, without any subterfuge, the sort who would find something to like in everyone. Hester found him easy to converse with, but good manners required that she not monopolize him. After a few minutes, she gave her attention to the dish before her while Petersham put a question to Miss Nolte. Becky was answering some remark of Derringham's, and Eversleigh was left free to talk with Hester.

"Have you heard from Rundle?" he asked quietly.

She looked up, startled. "Only this morning! How did you know?"

"No, don't look at me like that. I'm not omniscient, and I haven't been spying on you. I had a letter from him this morning, too, reminding me of my promise to help him sort through Stuart's papers."

She didn't mean to show her dismay so clearly, but he saw the expression in her eyes, and laughed. "Rundle holds me above suspicion, I'm afraid. And in my role of Justice of the Peace, he felt it would be quite proper for me to assist him. Would you prefer that I didn't?"

Hester was embarrassed and confused. She hardly knew how to answer him. "I'm sorry, my lord. It was only that I didn't realize you were a Justice. One of your brothers mentioned that you had spoken to a Justice shortly after Stuart's death, so..."

"Ah, that would be the squire. He's the Justice for the next county. Given the circumstances in which Stuart died, I felt it would be only proper to call him in. But once the coroner brought in a verdict of accidental death, I felt free to offer my services to Rundle. I fear you won't believe me, but my motives were pure. Rundle is getting up in age, and this business has upset him considerably. However, if it displeases you, I can withdraw my offer."

While Hester declaimed that it was not at all necessary, she thought that if he was truly a gentleman, he would withdraw his services without putting her in such an untenable position. He sat there, looking rather smug and, she fancied, laughing at her discomfort.

Miss Derringham, observing their exchange, rose abruptly, signalling to the ladies that it was time to withdraw, leaving the gentlemen to their cigars and brandy.

There was tangible tension in the room as the ladies seated themselves. Natalie Nolte tried to ease the strain by requesting Hermione to give them the pleasure of a song. Lady Petersham seconded the notion, and a somewhat mollified Hermione sat down in front of the spinet.

She played reasonably well, and was not at all averse to being the centre of attention. Hermione knew she presented a lovely and gracious figure as she sat poised before the keyboard, and she intended to remain there until the gentleman joined them. Her long fingers touched the ivory keys lightly, and then suddenly crashed down, producing a loud, discordant clamour. Hermione shrieked, and in her haste to get away from the spinet, overturned the bench.

The crash brought the gentlemen running. Eversleigh threw open the double doors and saw Hermione across the room, standing on top of a footstool, babbling loudly about some sort of creature in the spinet. Hester intuitively guessed what had occurred and edged closer to the instrument as Eversleigh moved to investigate. He looked into the spinet and briefly shared a grin with Petersham who stood beside him. Scooping out the offending creature, a tiny white mouse, he handed it over to a nervous footman, who rather reluctantly took it from the room.

Eversleigh went immediately to Hermione and helped her down. "I'm terribly sorry you were frightened, but it's only a harmless mouse—probably one of Jack's pets that must have got loose.''

''Got loose?'' she repeated, her voice rising. ''You know perfectly well that odious little brother of yours put it there deliberately. He *knew* I would play the spinet, and he did it on purpose! He should be severely punished!''

Eversleigh spoke quietly, hoping to soothe her. ''Be reasonable, Hermione. How could the boys convince a mouse to remain in the spinet all this time? It's been hours since they were in this room.''

Hester, who had spent too many years in close association with small boys to be easily convinced, peered closely into the spinet. As she'd suspected, there was evidence of crumbs, and what was left of a chunk of cheese. She surmised the mouse had been placed there earlier, and then well fed until it had fallen asleep. It probably didn't wake until Hermione had struck the first note. Had the boys calculated that Hermione would be the first to play, or was that only luck on their part? That it had been intended to scare Hermione she could easily believe.

Hermione would not be placated. Her nerves, she said, were positively shattered, and she demanded that her father take her home at once. ''Why, there might be more of those creatures in the room.'' She gave a convincing shudder as she looked round.

The other ladies, who had found the prank a trifle humorous, began peering about nervously, and the gathering broke up rapidly. Hester asked that someone be sent to the stables to inform Mulliken that they were ready to leave, and said her goodbyes.

Lord Eversleigh insisted on walking Becky and Hester to their carriage and attempted an apology of sorts. Hester quickly reassured him that she didn't regard one small mouse as cause for alarm. Their eyes met in mutual understanding, and he promised to call on her in the morning.

"That puts me in mind of something," she told him. "Would you bring with you the old journal that was found in the secret room? I should like to have a look at it."

Eversleigh studied her, his eyes turning cold. He answered without expression, "I assure you it was only an old book full of agricultural discussion and household hints."

"Yes, so Harry told me. But I should still like to have a look at it, if you've no objection."

"Very well. I shall return it tomorrow." He bade her good-night curtly and strode back to the house without another word.

CHAPTER SIX

HESTER SLEPT LATER than usual the following morning. Becky had kept her up late discussing the dinner party and Eversleigh's strange behaviour when he'd said good-night. Hester thought his manner had been odd, if not actually suspicious, while Becky maintained that he'd been angry. Though why he should have been angry with Hester was something she couldn't explain. Still, Becky remained staunch in her belief in him.

The dinner had done little to shed any light on their mystery. They now had three different offers to buy Silverdale—all from possible candidates for "Lord X," as Becky had dubbed their villain. Only Lord Derringham had refrained from trying to buy the estate. Becky found that suspicious in itself, and warned Hester to beware. It was always the person that one least suspected, she insisted, who turned out to be the villain.

Hester was still thinking over their conversation when Alice called urgently to her from down the hall. "Miss Hester, do come quick!"

She looked out the door of her room in time to see Alice duck back into the blue room, and hurried after her. When she entered, Alice was standing by the window, looking out intently.

"Whatever is the matter, Alice? You gave me a turn, shouting like that. I thought you'd hurt yourself."

"Oh, miss, do come look. It's Ben coming up the back way, and he looks something fearful. And he's carrying Blackie!"

Hester looked for herself. It *was* Ben, and he was staggering under the massive weight of her dog. She felt a little faint, for it looked as if they both had a good deal of blood on them, and Blackie's head was hanging limply from Ben's arms. She drew a deep breath and hurried down to the kitchen, calling for Becky as she went.

Mrs. Mulliken looked up as she flew through the kitchen, but Hester didn't pause for explanations. She worked the latch on the big door and got it opened just as Ben shouted for help. He stumbled in with his burden and, amid the cries of alarm, gently eased Blackie to the floor. The dog whimpered as he laid him down, and Ben looked up at them, blood and tears running together down his face.

"Someone shot him, Miss Hester! I found him about a half mile from here, barely crawling, but he was trying to reach home. Poor old boy. I carried him the rest of the way."

Stricken, Hester sank to the floor by the dog, unmindful of her dress. Becky, after one quick cry, ran to get linens and ointment. But Hester could see that it was going to take more than a bandage to help Blackie. His shoulder was ripped open, and he was losing a lot of blood.

As if reading her thoughts, Ben told her, "The horse doctor we use is Dr. Parsons, but he's away on holiday. I didn't know what else to do but bring him on home."

"You did just right, Ben. Now, would you take the carriage and see if you can find Dr. Layton. Tell him I need him at once."

"But, miss—he ain't no animal doctor!"

"He's dealt with bullet wounds before, and I'm sure he can deal with this one. Please, Ben, and hurry."

Ben looked at his wife in resignation, and with a shrug for the ways of the quality, set off to find the doctor. Mrs. Mulliken put the kettle on to boil, talking to herself all the while.

Hester refused to leave the dog and sat in the middle of the kitchen floor with Blackie's head in her lap. She kept a linen cloth pressed to the wound in an effort to stanch the flow of blood. She began to wonder if it was doing any good, as pad after pad became soaked through. Blackie looked at her with helpless eyes, unable to understand what had happened, and imploring her to help him somehow. She struggled not to cry as she whispered to him that he'd be all right. Hester sat there for over an hour, her muscles straining, and neither Mrs. Mulliken nor Becky dared to remonstrate with her. The only thing she asked for was a blanket to help keep the big dog warm while they waited.

When Dr. Layton finally arrived, he took one look at the mute appeal in Hester's eyes and forgot all the strictures he had intended for her ears. Before a bemused Ben, he knelt instead to have a look at the dog. He wasn't encouraging, but he promised Hester he'd try to get the ball out, and sew up the wound. The rest, he said, was in the hands of God.

The kitchen was quickly turned into an operating room. A long trestle table was cleared, and Ben and Layton between them lifted the dog up onto it. Ben brought some of the harness tack from the stables and with that they were able to strap Blackie down securely. A last strip of linen was bound securely around the dog's mouth in case he tried to bite. Hester would have liked to have fled the room, but Layton directed her to stand at the dog's head and speak quietly to him, while he was probing for the ball.

She managed to get through the ordeal without fainting, only by turning her eyes away from the doctor's exploring hands and concentrating on the inanities she was murmuring to the dog. The ball was not too deeply lodged and the doctor managed to extract it quickly, for which Hester was greatly thankful. He dusted the wound with basilicum powder and then bound it up.

While the doctor was working, Mrs. Mulliken made a comfortable pallet in the corner of her kitchen for Blackie. As soon as they finished, the men carried him to it, laying him down gently.

"If you can keep him quiet, and from biting off the bandages, he stands a fair chance of recovering," Layton told them. He added, for Mrs. Mulliken's benefit, "If it were Ben here, with a hole in his shoulder, I'd recommend some of your beef barley. But I've never prescribed for a dog before. See if he'll drink some broth for today, and tomorrow, if he wants some food, I should guess that it wouldn't harm him any."

"I don't know how to thank you, Dr. Layton," Hester said. "I realize it was presumptuous of me to ask you to attend Blackie, but I didn't know what else to do. I couldn't just let him die without trying..." Her words trailed off as tears came to her eyes, and the doctor, embarrassed, sought to change the subject.

"How did he come to be shot, anyway?" he asked gruffly. "I hope you haven't suffered another housebreaker?"

"No," Hester answered. "I suppose it must have been a poacher mistaking him for some wild animal."

"Ha! If it was a hunter, he was out after mighty big game with that kind of shot in his rifle!" Layton didn't see the ashen look on Hester's face as he gathered up his instruments, and he continued blithely, "More like, he was shot deliberate."

Becky showed the doctor out, and then insisted that Hester join her in the drawing room for a reviving glass of sherry. After she had settled Hester, she took her own seat and faced the girl. "Well, now, what are you thinking, my dear? Shouldn't we notify someone about the dog being shot?"

"Who? Lord Eversleigh? He's the Justice of the Peace," Hester replied sarcastically.

Becky ignored her tone. "I *do* think he should be told at once. I know you suspect him, Hester, but I cannot believe him capable of doing such a thing. To deliberately shoot an innocent dog down like that bespeaks a particularly vile-natured man. And you cannot have considered this through, Hester. Why, Lord Eversleigh could walk in here any time he wished without fear of Blackie."

Hester put up a hand to her aching head. "I can't think clearly. Nothing seems to make any sense. What you say is true of Eversleigh, but it also applies to our other suspects. Any of them could control Blackie, so why shoot him?" She stood up. "I think I'll go to my room and rest a bit. This has upset me so much, I declare I'm ready to pack up my bags and leave!"

"That's it!" Becky cried.

"What?"

"This was meant to scare us off! *That's* why Blackie was shot. Don't you see? Not because Lord X had any fear of him, but to put the fear in us!"

Hester stared at the brave little governess. "If I believed that were true, *nothing* would induce me to leave here!"

"I am extremely glad to hear you say so," Percival Mansfield drawled from the doorway. The ladies turned, startled by his sudden appearance. He strolled in, his attention fixed on straightening the ruffles at his wrists, and flicked an imaginary speck of dust from his coat. When he looked up and saw their astonishment, he apologized. "Do forgive me for walking in unannounced, but no one answered the door, although I knocked quite loudly several times. The door was a little ajar, and I could plainly hear voices, so I took the liberty of entering. I know I should have waited, and I would have if only the wind was not from the north. I find a northerly wind particularly hazardous to one of my delicate constitution. I am, alas, subject to frequent illness, if I do not take the proper precautions." Percy moved a little to the left of the window. "I fear you have a nasty draught coming in this window, Miss Martingale. You should have someone attend to that immediately."

Becky, after casting one contemptuous glance at him, left the room. Hester politely invited him to be seated and enquired if he cared for a cup of tea.

"It really would be most welcome, I confess. I don't believe anything to be more beneficial in warding off a chill than a nice cup of hot tea. But I shouldn't wish to put you to any trouble. Have the Mullikens abandoned you?"

Hester watched him closely as she replied, "No. An unfortunate accident occurred this morning, and they have been rather busy. Someone, a poacher most likely, mistook my dog for a wild animal and shot him."

"What? That huge mastiff? I admit he *looks* quite wild, but surely no one could mistake him for a deer or a rabbit! How very strange."

Conversation was halted for a moment as Alice brought in the tea tray. She set it down and quickly left. Hester thought, as she poured the tea, that Percy must not be a favourite with Mrs. Mulliken. There were none of her delicious little almond cakes or any fresh baked scones on the tray, but only a few dry biscuits. She handed him his cup and continued, "It was strange, but we were lucky and I have every hope that Blackie will recover. Dr. Layton was here and removed the shot from his shoulder, and the dog is in the kitchen now being tended to by the Mullikens."

"Ah, that explains why no one answered my knock. It appears I have not chosen a very propitious time to call. And if I heard you correctly when I came in, I am on a futile errand in any event."

"I'm afraid I don't understand you, sir."

He smiled, but it was without any warmth, and did not reach his narrow eyes. "I came at my father's request, Miss Martingale. He wished me to press forward his offer to buy Silverdale. However, since you are determined to remain here, I shall instead tell you how delighted I am. You make a charming, one might even say, exciting, addition to our countryside."

"Thank you, but you are too hasty in your conclusions. While I have no intention of leaving here *immediately*, I have not yet decided to stay indefinitely. You may tell your father that I am still considering his offer."

Percy daintily wiped his lips with a linen handkerchief before replying, "I am desolate. You would make a much more charming tenant than my ferret-faced cousin. But I must represent to you the urgency of my father's case. The lad is to be wed shortly. If we cannot hope to acquire Silverdale, another property must be found. We do not have the luxury of a great deal of time. Is there any hope you might reach a decision soon?"

"Very soon, I should think. Mr. Rundle, my cousin's solicitor, is on his way here. After he goes through Stuart's papers, I should have a better idea of how the estate is left."

"I see," Percy said, standing. "Well, I won't keep you any longer. Shall I tell my father you will send word as soon as possible?"

"Yes, of course." She rose also, and watched in considerable amusement as Percy prepared himself to brave the weather. First, a lavishly ornamented scarf was carefully wrapped round his throat. Then a fur-lined driving coat, with at least six capes, was donned. Leather driving gloves and a fur-trimmed beaver hat were added before Percy felt himself ready. Hester saw him out and watched after his carriage thoughtfully.

Less than an hour later, she was back at the door. This time it was to welcome Mr. Rundle, who arrived in a weather-beaten carriage which appeared to be as old as the solicitor himself. A hired post-boy assisted him with his valise, and there was some confusion until the charges were settled. At Hester's invitation, the white-haired gentleman sank gratefully into a chair. He was obviously tired from his journey, and Becky hovered about him offering him tea and an assortment of cakes.

"Or perhaps you would prefer a glass of sherry? My dear father, rest his soul, always had a drop of sherry after a journey. He said it restored his sense of balance."

"Thank you, dear lady," he said. "Tea will do nicely, but I know exactly what he meant. Carriages do have a way of jostling one about until you don't know if you're coming or going!" He went on to tell her of another experience, and Hester slipped quietly from the room.

It was apparent Mr. Rundle would not be up to discussing her cousin's affairs for some time, and she was anxious to visit Blackie. When she entered the kitchen, the dog lifted his head a little and gave an excited bark. His tail beat a tattoo on the floor, and while he was definitely looking better, he was still too weak to sit up. She knelt beside him, and Blackie gratefully licked her fingers.

"His eyes are much brighter, miss," Ben pointed out. "My guess is he'll be trying to get up tomorrow. Then we'll have a rare time trying to keep him quiet."

"I'm so glad," she said, rising. "Ben, I didn't wish to alarm the others, but if Blackie was shot intentionally, it might be well to have someone on the watch tonight. Do you think, if you got a few hours' sleep directly after dinner, that you could stay up tonight?"

"I was thinking the same thing, miss, and don't you be fretting. No one will get into this house without Ben E. Mulliken knowing it!"

Hester thanked him and returned to the drawing room. Lord Eversleigh had arrived during her absence, and he greeted her more pleasantly than she had expected.

"The truth is," he told her with a disarming smile, "I'm feeling very *de trop* here. Rundle has cut me out with Miss Becky."

Hester glanced at her companion, totally absorbed in her conversation with Mr. Rundle, and laughed. It was apparent that the older couple was oblivious of her presence.

Eversleigh reclaimed her attention. "I've brought the book you wished to see, though I'm hurt you wouldn't take my word that it's a harmless farming journal."

Really, the man had the most disconcerting habit of voicing matters better left unspoken. She felt a blush suffusing her cheeks, and tried to dissemble. "It's not a question of accepting your word, sir. I merely wished to see the journal for myself."

"Having a keen interest in matters agricultural?" he quizzed her.

She returned no answer as she accepted the proffered book and laid it aside for examination later. "Actually, I'm glad you called. There is another matter that I feel…that Becky feels you should know about." *Drat the man.* He had her stumbling over her words like a tongue-tied school miss.

"And what does *Miss Becky* feel I should know?"

"That Blackie was deliberately shot this morning!" She watched with satisfaction as his smile disappeared, and then immediately felt contrite as she read the concern in his eyes, concern that seemed all too real. She hastened to reassure him. "He's recovering in the kitchen now. Dr. Layton removed the ball from his shoulder this morning, and he thinks that if we can only keep him quiet, he'll be fine."

Eversleigh digested this without comment, and then a look of unholy mirth crossed his features. "Did you say *Dr. Layton* removed the ball? From a dog?"

"Well, yes. Only because Dr. Parsons is away, and I didn't know what else to do but call him in. He was very kind."

"Oh, how I shall roast him for this!"

"No, no—you mustn't! Not when he has been so good." Without thinking, she impulsively laid a hand beseechingly upon his sleeve.

He looked down at her hand and then into her eyes. "One would not think it to look at you, but obviously you have great powers of persuasion. I shall have to take care in my dealings with you."

She hastily removed her hand. "You miss the point, Lord Eversleigh. Blackie was shot for a specific purpose. At least, Dr. Layton thinks so, judging from the kind of shot that was used. Becky believes that someone is trying to frighten us away."

"That is certainly a possibility. Very well. I shall send Zack and Tobias Hawkins down to patrol your property. Ben knows them both, and will trust them to keep an eye out."

She reluctantly agreed, and then conscientiously made haste to thank him. He waved her off, and Hester changed the subject, asking him with a grin, "Did you discover how the mouse got into the spinet?"

Eversleigh laughed. "Harry and Jack both swear their innocence, and I'm almost inclined to believe them. Still, it's hard to credit that a mouse just happened to crawl inside the spinet, carrying his own hunk of cheese. I fear Hermione will never forgive me."

"She was dreadfully upset. I think it really frightened her. I have sometimes observed that some ladies, who otherwise are very courageous, have an unreasonable fear of small creatures like mice and frogs."

"But not you, Miss Martingale?"

"Oh, no. I spent far too many years in the company of small boys to be afraid of harmless creatures. My particular bugbear is fire."

"Fire?" He glanced at the coals steadily burning in the grate. "I thought you enjoyed a cozy fire on a chilly afternoon."

"So I do. That's a different thing entirely. My fear is of burning buildings—of being trapped inside."

Becky interrupted them. "Excuse me, Hester, but I think I should show our guest to his room and give him a chance to rest a bit before dinner."

"I'm afraid age has its drawbacks, Miss Martingale," the solicitor added. "Time was, I could travel all day and still do a fair amount of work." He turned to Eversleigh, extending his hand. "Charles, it's always a pleasure to see you. Will you be giving me a hand tomorrow?"

Eversleigh agreed, and with that settled, Becky possessively led their guest from the room. Eversleigh started to take his leave also, but Hester detained him.

"If you are coming to assist Mr. Rundle tomorrow, perhaps Jennifer could come with you? And the boys, also?"

"They don't deserve such a treat, but if Miss Fontaine will give them leave, I'll bring them. Now, don't bother showing me out. I'm going to go by the kitchen and have a word with Ben about the guards before I leave."

She stayed in the drawing room after he had gone and idly picked up the book he'd returned. It appeared to be, as he had said, merely an old agricultural journal, interspersed with household hints. Her eyes skimmed over foreign phrases and references to such mundane matters as underdraining and embanking. A recipe for A Better Pickled Beef did little to hold her attention, and she continued to leaf through the book. Then she noticed the missing pages. Ragged edges showed where several pages had been torn from the binding.

Her headache returned as she considered their significance. Eversleigh could have found something incriminating to himself and removed the pages. He had been vexed with her when she insisted upon its return, and then quite nonchalant about it this morning. Of course it was also just possible that the pages had been missing before Eversleigh had taken the book.

The missing pages weighed heavily on her mind the rest of the day. She still had not come to any conclusion when the Eversleighs arrived the next afternoon. Jack was looking very healthy, except for his arm, which, for once, was properly supported by his sling. He asked at once how

Blackie was doing. Eversleigh told her, *sotto voce*, that Jack considered himself and Blackie to be kindred spirits, having both been, in a manner of speaking, wounded.

Alice bore the boys off to see the dog for themselves, listening with considerable relish as the boys planned the dire fate of the scoundrel who had dared to shoot Blackie. Hester shared a smile with Eversleigh over their bloodthirsty natures before taking Jenny up to her room.

"I know you want to see Blackie, too, and you shall shortly. First, I have a surprise for you. Becky and I were tidying up the attics when I came across something I think you might like. Now close your eyes."

The little girl sat on the edge of the rocking chair and squeezed her eyes tightly shut, holding out both hands in expectation.

"Keep your eyes shut," Hester warned as she crossed to the wardrobe and removed a doll. It was close to eighteen inches long, and dressed in an elaborate gown of thin silk, with the skirt looped up by tape-ties inside. The front was cut in a square neckline with an intricately laced stomacher setting it off. A wide hoop held the skirt out, and tiny brocade slippers showed beneath it, fastened over the foot with oval buckles. The doll was a fashion-plate, and Hester guessed her to be about thirty years old. The blond hair was piled high in woven curls, and traces of powder still remained. She laid the doll gently in Jenny's waiting arms.

The child opened her eyes and, looking from the doll to Hester, asked "Are you giving her to me? Is she really mine?"

"Yes, she's yours. I had a doll almost like her when I was your age. I called her Mademoiselle DuBarry, and she went everywhere with me."

Jenny touched the doll lovingly and smoothed out the faded rose skirt. "What happened to your doll?"

For an instant, Hester recalled the flames that had engulfed her home. Her parents had died in that fire, and almost all their possessions had been burned, including her doll. She shook off the choking feeling the memories evoked, and tried for a light tone. "I'm not really sure—it was a long time ago."

Jenny, catching the fleeting look of sadness on her friend's face sought to comfort her. "Perhaps she's in heaven, like my mother."

"Now there's a good thought, and you're probably right. What are you going to name your doll?"

"Mademoiselle DuBarry," she replied without hesitation, "and I shall take her everywhere with me—except perhaps to church."

"There's one thing about Mademoiselle you must remember, Jenny. She is a lady, and *always* minds her manners. She won't like it a bit if you don't mind yours."

Jenny nodded solemnly. "My mother used to make me mind my manners."

"Well, now you have Mademoiselle, and she'll be very displeased if you are rude, or do something like…oh, like putting your brother's mouse in the spinet."

Jenny's mouth formed a tiny oval of surprise. "How did you know? Even Charlie didn't guess!"

"That's a secret. However, if you do such a thing again, I'll know, and so will Mademoiselle. And if you displease her, she'll have to come back and live with me. Is that understood?"

Jenny held her doll tighter and nodded in shy agreement. "May I go show Mademoiselle to Charlie?"

"I'm afraid your brother's a trifle busy just now. Why don't we wait until we have tea?"

Jenny reluctantly and impatiently waited. Not even a visit to Blackie had the power to distract her for long. She left her brothers playing with the dog and took her doll into the drawing room to wait for tea. As soon as Eversleigh and Rundle appeared, she jumped up and ran to show them her treasure.

After Charles had obligingly made a fuss over the doll, and Mademoiselle had been given her own place on the settee, attention was focused on the tray Mrs. Mulliken brought them. It was laden with cakes and tarts wafting their delicious aroma across the room. When everyone had been served, Hester asked Rundle if he was making any progress.

"Very little," he sighed. "I fear I've never seen a more tangled mishmash than the condition of your cousin's papers. There is no order," he told them plaintively, clearly shocked by this further evidence of Stuart's lack of character. "I don't know how I should manage without Charles's assistance, and, of course, that of dear Miss Becky. She has been invaluable." A smile lightened his countenance as he looked fondly at Miss Beckles, and he seemed to forget that anyone else was present.

Becky seemed pleased at the compliment, a trace of colour coming into her cheeks. Her bright eyes returned Rundle's regard, full of approval. Hester, watching her companion, tried not to stare. She glanced at Eversleigh, and then quickly looked away as he distinctly winked at her. When she dared to look up again, he appeared perfectly serious, giving Harry his undivided attention.

Alice tapped on the door to announce an unexpected visitor, and Dr. Layton was shown in. If he was surprised at finding such a large and merry group, he gave no indication of it, and greeted them all cordially. The reason for his call was to look in on Blackie, but he was reluctant to mention that in front of Lord Eversleigh.

"I was driving down the lane, when I got a whiff of Mrs. Mulliken's pastries. That tantalizing aroma is drifting about, an unfair temptation to those going about their lawful business."

Hester and Becky both invited him to join them for tea, and a place was quickly made for him. Eversleigh watched amusedly and at length commented lazily, "I thought you might be stopping to enquire about your patient's progress."

"Ah, well it wouldn't do any harm to have a look at that arm while I'm here. How's it feeling, Jack?"

Eversleigh would not be diverted. "I wasn't referring to Jack, Doctor. I was talking about your *other* patient. I understand you performed quite an operation on Blackie yesterday."

"Oh, that. It wasn't anything. Poor dog had a ball in his shoulder, and I did what I could to help Miss Martingale."

"Too modest by half. The eminent Dr. Josiah Layton, physician to Royalty, demeaning himself to operate on a mere dog! I wonder how the Regent will feel when he learns a physician who attended him at Brighton is now giving succour to dogs."

"And I suppose you would have refused to do what you could for the animal, had you been here?"

"Not at all. But I am hardly an eminent physician. And when I think how you complained about having my boys as patients..."

"Let me tell you, Eversleigh, that dog is a far better patient than any of your hare-brained brothers! Just look at Jack there with his arm out of the sling again."

Jack hastily restored his arm to the sling, and Hester roundly defended the doctor. "You must know how indebted I am to Dr. Layton, for I'm very sure Blackie would have died without his help, and it is unkind of you, Lord Eversleigh, to roast him for such a generous deed!" She turned to Layton, saying, "Blackie is much improved. Would you care to come out to the kitchen and see how well he does?"

The doctor readily joined her and escorted her from the room, with a last backward glance for Eversleigh, which could only be termed a smirk. Once out of earshot, however, he advised her, "Don't pay any mind to Eversleigh. For all his levity, he's a good man, and no one I'd rather have beside me in a difficult corner."

Hester ignored this and entered the kitchen ahead of him. Blackie was chewing at his bandage, and she scolded him. He immediately put his head down on his paws and looked up at her with the mournful air of an animal about to be beaten unjustly. He allowed Layton to examine him, licking his hand once or twice. "I think he'll be fine," the doctor announced, "but that bandage needs to stay on for a few days. Perhaps an old ham bone would distract him."

Mrs. Mulliken provided one, and it proved effective. Blackie instantly abandoned chewing on the bandage in favour of the bone. But Mrs. Mulliken warned her, "If I have to keep that animal in bones until the bandage comes off, we'll be eaten out of house and home!"

Layton would not return to the drawing room with her, claiming he was pressed for time, and Hester walked with him to the door. "Dr. Layton, do you remember when you left yesterday morning—when Becky showed you out?"

"Yes, why do you ask?"

"I wonder if you recall whether she shut the door securely? We had a visitor, shortly after you left, who said the door was ajar."

"I suppose I should not ask who the visitor was. Well, one thing I can tell you is that she did close the door— slammed it, in fact. There was a slight breeze, and it must have caught the door. I had just turned back to tell her that I would look in today when the door slammed."

Hester considered this, but offered no further explanation, and the doctor took his leave wondering what was afoot. Perhaps Eversleigh would tell him later.

CHAPTER SEVEN

THE DAYS WHICH FOLLOWED evolved into a pleasant pattern, and for long stretches, Hester actually forgot the riddle Stuart had bequeathed to her. She had, with Alice's devoted assistance, discovered a hoard of treasures squirrelled away in the old attics. She confided to Becky that it was little wonder Stuart had been run off his legs. It seemed every item that had needed the least mending or repair had been consigned to the attics and left there.

"I'm not at all surprised, dear. Oliver told me that your cousin never possessed the slightest notion of economy. And he never paid the smallest heed to Oliver's advice, which I'm certain was excellent," Becky replied absently.

Hester had made no comment when Becky had suddenly altered her mode of referring to their solicitor from "dear Mr. Rundle" to "Oliver," but she now eyed her companion with mingled humour and apprehension. "Why, Becky, I do believe you're developing a tendre for Mr. Rundle."

"What nonsense you're talking, Hester," she said, although the colour rising in her cheeks gave the lie to her words. "At my age, one is past all that, even if it's not to be wondered at if I do hold Oliver in esteem. Such delightful looks. White hair always makes a gentleman look so distinguished, don't you agree?"

Hester replied gravely, "I see. I'm glad to know you haven't a tendre for him. Becky, has he said anything about the estate?"

"No... only, I fear the worst. Oliver has been extremely severe in his criticism of Stuart's management. And I must say that it does seem the more papers we catalogue, the more bills we find, and not one of them with a notation of what's been paid, and what may still be owing."

"From what I have learned about my cousin, it's doubtful that anything was paid. He apparently was one of those foolish young men who deem it a waste of good blunt to settle one's accounts."

Becky sadly agreed with her, and then, on hearing Rundle coming down the stairs, quickly excused herself. "I'll just see if Oliver has everything he needs. He's not at all finicky, you know, but he is nice in his tastes, and likes his tea just so."

Hester smiled as she watched Becky bustle from the room. Her old governess was looking much better of late. Partly, she suspected, from Mrs. Mulliken's superb cooking, and partly from the considerable amount of attention Rundle was paying her. She knew she wouldn't see Becky again before tea-time, for he and Becky would remain closeted in the library until four o'clock. Lord Eversleigh generally joined them around one, and claimed tea as his reward for the afternoon's work. The younger Eversleighs appeared on her doorstep at three. The boys spent the hour before tea exercising Blackie, and Jenny considered that hour as her private time with Hester.

It was a cheerful and ravenous group that converged on the drawing room each afternoon, much to Mrs. Mulliken's delight. And most afternoons, Dr. Layton also managed to find himself in the vicinity of Silverdale just at tea-time. Even Blackie was allowed to join the party, and Dr. Layton kept a possessive eye on him.

That afternoon, when Jack and Harry brought the huge dog in, Layton looked him over critically, and advised the boys to go easy with the exercise for a few more days.

Lord Eversleigh, lounging at his ease in one of the wing-chairs, mocked him, "I'm amazed that you show more concern over that mongrel than you ever did over any of us."

"Very likely," Layton agreed. "He's a better patient. For one thing, he don't argue, which is more than I can say for any of your brood. Maybe Parsons is smarter than I gave him credit for. There's something to be said for working with mongrels."

"He's not a mongrel!" Jack glared up defensively. "He's a full-bred mastiff, and even the Prince Regent keeps mastiffs at the Pavilion."

"Yes, but I'm sure that not even Prinny's dogs are allowed to eat a whole dish of macaroons," Eversleigh drawled. "Harry, move that plate before he has them all. Did Miss Martingale tell you, Layton, that Parsons came by yesterday and declared you did a very creditable job? In fact, he said he'd be glad to take you on as an assistant."

"If I have many more days like this one, I'm likely to take him up on his offer. Derringham had me in this morning. He's suffering from gout again, though what can he expect, the way he eats! What good it does for me to see him when he won't follow my advice is beyond my comprehension. And Hermione was in a rare taking, which didn't improve his temper any."

"What was upsetting Miss Derringham?" Becky asked sweetly. "Did she see another mouse?"

Eversleigh laughed appreciatively, as she had intended, and she even drew a reluctant smile from the doctor, before he answered, "I don't believe so, but she didn't confide in me. I came in just as she threw a book at her maid. Nasty temper that woman has. Don't let her get her claws in you, Charles, or you'll never know another minute's peace."

Harry, Jack and Jennifer looked anxiously at their brother, hoping for a stout denial. Hester and Becky busied themselves with teacups, pretending, unsuccessfully, not to have heard Layton's remark, while Eversleigh merely gazed at the doctor, a half smile on his lips.

Dr. Layton, uncomfortably aware of the solecism he had committed in speaking so freely, stammered a retraction of sorts, and added, "I suppose you think I should not have said that, and you're in the right of it, of course. It's only that I'm tired and spoke without thinking. Mrs. Rivington kept me up half the night before she gave birth to twins."

The subject of Hermione Derringham was allowed to drop, to the disappointment of almost everyone. The ladies obligingly asked several questions about the Rivington babes, and the well-being of the mother. It wasn't until Dr. Layton took his leave that anything more was said about Hermione. He asked Eversleigh to walk with him to his carriage, and when they were alone on the drive, attempted once more to apologize.

"Charles, I'm truly sorry I let my tongue run away with me. Didn't mean to put you on the spot like that, but the thing is, Hermione's found out you've been here every afternoon and she's buzzing about like a mad hornet. Aye, smile if you like, but she's got her cap set for you, and she won't rest until she's got you. Mark my words."

Eversleigh clapped him lightly on the shoulder. "You're working yourself into a tizzy over nothing. There's no way Hermione can force me into marriage, you know. How many times have you railed at me for being an obstinate, stubborn mule who only does what he pleases? Rest easy, old friend. Hermione's been catching cold at this game for years."

"Humph. Well, I warned you, and I can't do more than that," Layton muttered, climbing into his carriage. When he was comfortably seated, and had the reins in hand, he added, "You take my advice all the same and stay out of her way. Better men than you have found themselves caught in parson's mousetrap."

Eversleigh watched as the doctor gave his horses the office to start, and tooled smartly down the drive. He lifted a hand in salute, remarking so softly that only a clump of dahlias heard him, "I hope you may wish me happy soon, but it will be with a very different lady than Hermione."

He strolled back to the house and encountered Hester in the hall, just coming down the stairs. She stopped a few steps from the bottom and leaned over the banister. Her mouth wore a prim look, but her eyes were brimming with laughter.

"Poor Dr. Layton. I never thought to see him so flustered. I do hope you reassured him?"

"That his *faux pas* was not beyond forgiveness, or that my matrimonial plans do not include Miss Derringham?" He stood just below her and watched the emotions fly across her face.

His question caught her off balance. She tilted her tiny chin up in her own determined fashion and answered saucily, "I'm sure it can be no concern of mine whom you choose to wed." She continued down the steps just as he moved to the foot of the stairs, and she faced him squarely. "Of course I was referring to Dr. Layton, and I do hope you set him at ease. We enjoy his visits here, and I should not like him made to feel uncomfortable."

"Ten to one he'll have dismissed the entire incident from his mind. But have you no curiosity, Miss Martingale? Or interest in my plans?" He was standing so close that Hester could see each individual lash curling over his green eyes, and a tiny pulse beating in his temple. His compelling gaze held her still, and she felt almost as if she were suffocating, so hard was it to get her breath. His hand reached up to her, and then as quickly fell to his side as Harry and Jack erupted from the drawing room.

"Charlie, Miss Becky invited us to stay for dinner if you'll allow it. Say yes, Charlie, please?"

Eversleigh turned to face his brothers, and put an arm about Jack's shoulders. "Sorry, fellows, but we've dinner waiting for us at home. Harry, go and find your sister."

Although his tone was neither rough nor stern, the boys knew instantly that he would brook no argument. Harry went dejectedly in search of Jenny, and Jack made only a token protest with an oblique reference to the dessert Mrs. Mulliken had promised him.

When the party from the manor had taken their leave, the house seemed unnaturally quiet. Dinner passed with only the most desultory conversation, and as soon as it was polite to do so, Rundle excused himself. He returned to the library, trying to get as much accomplished as he could. He was well aware that settling Stuart's estate was taking more of his time than he should allow, and although he wasn't anxious to return to the city, he felt that was where his duty lay. Becky was assisting him, and she, too, was unusually quiet. The news that Rundle hoped to complete his task by the end of the week had depressed her spirits more than she cared to admit.

Hester, left to her own devices, devoted the evening to mending one of the larger tablecloths. She took her sewing into the library with Becky and Rundle and settled before the fire. She was paying scant attention to the conversation of the others, her mind dwelling on the incomprehensible Lord Eversleigh. Stubbornly, she refused to think more of him and tried to fix her mind on plans for the next day. Provokingly, her wayward thoughts kept returning to Eversleigh. Hester was about to cast her stitchery aside and seek out an engrossing book when Rundle startled her with a loud exclamation.

"This is very strange, indeed! Becky, come and see what you make of this," Rundle said, showing her a piece of wrinkled foolscap.

Becky obligingly read the few lines of the script and looked up in confusion. "It appears to be something Stuart paid out, but what?"

Hester, her interest caught, got up to have a look. It was difficult to make out the scrawling handwriting, but she instantly recognized it as her cousin's. She read aloud, "The Ram's Head, Logenberry, fifty pounds."

"That's what I made it out to be, Miss Martingale, but I never heard of The Ram's Head, nor of a Logenberry. At least, it looks as though this is one item your cousin paid," Rundle told her, taking the note back.

"Yes, and that makes me curious. Why should he pay this when he wasn't being dunned for it? Unless perhaps it was a wager?"

"Very likely," Becky agreed, "and Ram's Head could be the name of a horse. Or perhaps Logenberry was the horse. I believe they often have strange names like that."

"It's possible," Hester said, her forehead creased in thought. "But Logenberry sounds like a man's name, and The Ram's Head more like an inn or tavern. I wonder if there's such a place. Maybe Ben would know."

"You ask him, Miss Martingale, and in the meantime I'll hold on to this note and we'll see what Lord Eversleigh thinks of it tomorrow." Rundle put the note aside, reposing complete faith in his friend's ability to sort it out. Hester, who could not condone his willingness simply to hand everything over to Eversleigh, kept her own counsel. But at the first opportunity she excused herself and went in search of Ben Mulliken.

She found him in the kitchen with his wife, a large slice of cherry pie set before him. He stood up and hastily wiped the crumbs from his mouth before asking what he could do for her. Hester told him about the note they'd found, and her conclusions.

"Think, Ben, have you ever seen a tavern or inn by that name? Or does Logenberry mean anything to you?"

He shook his head slowly, "Can't say as it does, Miss Hester. But I can ask about tomorrow. Mayhap someone at The White Hart would know. I'll drop in, casual like, and see what I can learn."

Mrs. Mulliken nodded her head, as if in agreement, and added, "You should ask his lordship about it, miss. If anyone were to know, Lord Eversleigh would."

Hester managed to thank them and retire to her room without revealing her annoyance. It was amazing, she thought, how these simple country people looked on Eversleigh as some sort of demigod, capable of solving their every problem. Even Hermione Derringham: now there was a woman one would expect to look down on any man who was not a Town tulip, but if Dr. Layton was to be believed, even she had set her cap for Eversleigh.

Hester fumed on the follies of the female sex as she brushed out her hair. If a man had wealth and a title to recommend him, his faults would be willingly overlooked. He could be obese and addicted to gaming or drink and still be considered a fine catch by the ton. Of course, she conceded, Eversleigh was far from obese. If one was fair, one would admit that he was, in fact, quite handsome. And he certainly possessed a rapier-sharp mind. She suspected that beneath the lazy facade he chose to present, he could be quite dangerous, perhaps even ruthless.

Hester laid the brush aside and looked out the window. The drive was bathed in moonlight, and she decided it must have been affecting her senses. Drawing the shutters closed, she laughed at herself, but moonlight or no, she promised herself to be on guard against Eversleigh. The man had a devastating charm. He'd caught her off balance that afternoon. She must not allow him to do so again.

Accordingly, Hester was noticeably cool towards him when he joined them for tea the following day. Becky and Rundle carried the conversation, with ready assistance from the children. The occasional conversational gambits directed to Hester were answered in monosyllables, which seemed to afford Eversleigh a great deal of amusement.

When the doors to the drawing room opened, she rose in relief, thinking Layton had finally arrived. Hester managed to cover her surprise as Hermione Derringham was shown in, and greeted her with tolerable composure. "Miss Derringham, how pleasant. Do come in. You know Lord Eversleigh, of course, and this is Mr. Rundle, my cousin's solicitor."

"Oh, yes," she said, tapping him playfully on the arm. "You're the gentleman that's keeping poor Charles occupied every afternoon looking through those dusty papers of Stuart's. I don't know whether I shall forgive you for that."

"Well, he did volunteer to assist me—"

"Yes, and I can see how terribly hard you're both working," she interrupted with an arch glance for Eversleigh.

"Looks are often deceptive, Hermione," Eversleigh intervened. "This tea is our reward for a very tedious afternoon."

"How dreadful for you, Charles. I do hope you'll be finished soon, so we can resume our afternoon rides?"

Rundle opened his mouth to speak, but Eversleigh forestalled him. "It's difficult to say at this point. But how is it that you are still here? I'd thought you would have returned to London by now."

"What? And leave you to rusticate all alone? I would not be so cruel." She turned her attention to the boys. "How are you, Richard? Are you behaving yourself?"

Harry answered her politely, not bothering to correct her, and then asked if he and his brother could be excused. Eversleigh nodded, and Hermione turned her attention to Jennifer.

"That's a very pretty doll you have. Though I must say she is sadly out of style. How would you like me to bring you a new doll? I have one who is wearing one of the latest fashions, just shipped over from France."

"No!" Jenny cried vehemently, clutching her own doll tightly. She realized as Hermione drew back in shocked surprise that she had been uncivil again and added conscientiously, "I'm sorry, Miss Derringham, but Mademoiselle DuBarry is my *friend*. She's not just a doll. But it was kind of you to offer.''

Hester intervened, touched by the dignity of the child in her attempt to behave politely. She enquired of Hermione how Lord Derringham was faring, which led to an animated discussion of the gout, and the stubbornness of males afflicted with the malady, until it was generally agreed that most men had little regard for their health. Lord Eversleigh, an excellent specimen of physical well-being, kept silent, and Rundle, too, was strangely quiet.

When the conversation began to lag, Eversleigh took the opportunity to take his leave, and Hermione suddenly remembered the time. "Oh, dear, I hadn't meant to visit for so long. Papa will be thinking I've overturned my curricle and sending out search parties for me. I really must fly. Charles, will you walk with me to my carriage?'' She bade the ladies a brief goodbye, utterly ignoring Jenny and Mr. Rundle. There was silence until the doors closed behind her, and Becky could not contain herself any longer. "Well! I never saw a more brazen display. What an encroaching female.''

Hester tried futilely to quiet her, uncomfortably aware of Jenny's rapt attention, but Becky would not be silenced. "Eversleigh may say what he will, but even a blind man could see Dr. Layton was right.''

"Speaking of Dr. Layton,'' Hester interrupted, "I wonder what detained him today.''

Eversleigh returned as she finished speaking, and she looked to him almost thankfully. "We were just discussing Dr. Layton, and wondering what could have occurred to prevent him from joining us today.''

"Were you?'' One eyebrow rose skeptically. "I thought you'd be discussing quite a different matter, but neither is of any real importance. I regret that Hermione disturbed our tea, for I wished to speak with you particularly about your legacy. Unfortunately, there are matters on my estate that require my immediate attention, and I really must take my leave. However, I know you will be delighted to learn that we should be finished with all the paperwork by Friday."

"And...?" Hester prompted.

"And—" he smiled, drawing out the syllable "—you may live quite comfortably at Silverdale for as long as it pleases you."

"Oh, Miss Hester, now you won't have to go away," Jenny cried. "I'm so glad."

"So are we all," her brother agreed, "but now we must get home. We can discuss this further tomorrow."

Becky and Hester both began talking at once and throwing questions at him until he held up his hands in mock self-defence, and they laughed. Hester hugged Jenny, and then Becky, and politely extended her hand to Eversleigh. "Forgive us, Lord Eversleigh, but your news comes as such a shock, albeit a pleasant one. I was under the impression that I would be more likely to owe on the estate than to benefit from it. How came this about?"

"I haven't time to discuss the details now, but Rundle will explain it all to you. For the present, just enjoy your good fortune."

She withdrew her hand shyly and tried to thank him. He waved her gratitude aside, and she was about to show him out when Rundle recalled the memorandum he had found. There was more delay while he fetched the note for Eversleigh, and they all waited anxiously while he read it.

"What do you make of it, Charles?" Rundle asked.

"Nothing as yet, but it certainly bears looking into," he replied, still studying the slip of paper. Looking up, he asked Hester, "Would you object if I kept this tonight? I'd like to study it further."

She found herself readily agreeing, without quite knowing why. After he had gone, she wondered what had possessed her to hand over her first real clue. She intended to learn what she could about the note herself, without Eversleigh's assistance. However, honesty forced her to admit that it had completely slipped her mind. She was determined, before she forgot again, to see if Ben had learned anything. Hester promised Becky she would return in a few moments and left her companion with Rundle.

As soon as they were alone, Becky challenged the solicitor. She stood, arms akimbo, and told him, "You heed me, Oliver Rundle. I've worked with you every day on Stuart's papers and there hasn't been a thing to indicate that Hester would inherit anything but a great load of debt. Now suddenly Lord Eversleigh is telling the child she can live quite comfortably here for as long as she pleases. Hester is the nearest thing to a daughter I have, and I won't have—"

"Becky, you are needlessly concerned. There are circumstances which have...have altered the situation...matters that only came to my attention this afternoon."

"Is that what Eversleigh wished to discuss with you in private?"

Before he could answer, Hester returned, in high gig and anxious to discuss the details of her good fortune. She addressed Rundle with a smile and a lightness in her voice that Becky had not heard for some time.

"This certainly has been a day of surprises. From everything Becky told me, I had resigned myself to expect very little. In fact, I was convinced I should have to sell this house. To what do I owe my sudden wealth?"

"I wouldn't term it *wealth*, precisely," Rundle said, hedging.

"Oh, I daresay it may not seem much to you, but if it is sufficient to enable me to live here comfortably, I assure you I shall regard it as a fortune. You see, I haven't had a home of my own since I was a young girl. Now tell me, shall I be enough beforehand with the world to employ the Mullikens?"

"Why, yes, of course, and your maid, as well. While I don't know the exact extent of your income yet, I am certain it will be ample enough to cover all your needs."

Hester did a little jig and hugged Becky. "This is too good to be true! I intend to hear all the details from you, sir. I promise you I want to know everything! But first I must go and talk with Mrs. Mulliken and Alice, too."

Rundle stood up abruptly. "Then if you'll excuse me, I believe I should rest a bit before dinner." He was determined not to be left alone with Becky for an inquisition. He held the door open for Hester and, with a quick glance over his shoulder, followed her out before Becky had time to reproach him. She let him leave without protest, thinking he could not avoid her for long in so small a house. She remained in the salon for a few minutes, considering his odd behaviour. Unable to come to any conclusion, she soon gave it up and went in search of Hester.

Becky heard voices coming from the kitchen and entered to find Mrs. Mulliken seated at the long table, her apron pulled up about her face, and heaving great sobs. Ben stood behind his wife, patting her uselessly on the shoulder and urging her to stop crying. Hester explained to Becky, "I've just been telling them the good news."

"Of course. I can see it's cheered her up something wonderful."

Mrs. Mulliken gulped and wiped at her eyes. "I'm that sorry to be going all to pieces like this, miss, but we never expected you'd be able to stay on here, much less be willing to keep us on."

"What? Not keep the best cook in the entire country? Why, I shall be the envy of the neighbourhood. Even Lord Eversleigh swore he'd discharge his fancy French chef if you'd come to the manor house and cook for him."

"Yes, miss," she said with a sniff, regaining a little composure. "And he did offer us a place when Mr. Stuart died. But Ben and me, we like Silverdale. It's been our home for so long. I know every nook and cranny in this kitchen, and I don't mind telling you, I was fair dreading leaving it."

"Then we'll consider the matter settled. You and Ben will stay on, and Alice, too. And I want you to find a suitable girl from the village to help you with the heavy work."

The older woman looked up with touching gratitude. She and Becky smiled at her pleasure and left her with Ben, discussing whether Sarah Gibbons's oldest daughter might be trained for kitchen work.

They returned to the drawing room and had just settled themselves when Alice came in search of them, bearing a message from Rundle. "He says he's feeling poorly, Miss Hester, and maybe he could have a tray in his room for dinner?"

Hester was full of instant concern. "Should I go up to him, or perhaps send for Dr. Layton?"

Becky put a restraining hand on her arm and calmed her. "I'm sure it's just a bilious attack. Oliver told me he gets them frequently, and I think it would only make him uncomfortable if we made a fuss. Mrs. Mulliken can fix him something light and take it up. I'm sure he'll be much better by morning."

Hester looked dubious, but Becky's calmness served to reassure her. She knew her companion doted on Rundle, and if *she* was not upset, clearly there was no reason to worry.

BECKY WAS PROVED CORRECT the next morning. Oliver Rundle came downstairs for breakfast, and if he hesitated at the door of the morning room, it was only a matter of seconds before he squared his shoulders and walked in. He greeted both ladies cheerfully, and to Hester's expressed concern, he replied he was feeling much more the thing.

"I'm so glad," Hester told him in all sincerity. "I should hate to think you made yourself ill with all the tedious work you've done on my behalf. I shall never be able to thank you enough. And I must say, we're going to miss you sorely when you go back to London. Are you set on leaving tomorrow?"

"Regrettably so. I fear I've been away far too long as it is. You and Becky have made my stay so pleasant that London seems far away. Almost another world, and vastly unappealing just now." He looked at Becky, but she would not meet his eyes. Hester watched them with interest, but Becky was preoccupied with buttering her toast and seemed disinclined to speak.

"I hope you don't intend to desert us once Stuart's affairs are settled. You must find time to come and visit us this summer."

"Thank you, Miss Hester. It's exceedingly kind of you."

Again, Hester waited for her companion to speak, and when she did not, Hester filled the awkward silence with the first thought that came to mind. "You know, dear sir, I was so excited last evening that I never did ask you the source of my sudden income."

Rundle was ready for her question. He noted he had Becky's full attention now, and cleared his throat. "Lord Eversleigh is the one who's really responsible. He knew your uncle had invested heavily in the Funds years ago. I knew that, also, of course, but I assumed that Stuart had long since sold out. Do you recall when Wellington defeated Bonaparte? Well, before news of the victory reached London, there were a number of disturbing rumours afoot that Wellington had been beaten. Everyone who could, or so it seemed, was rushing to sell out of the Funds, and a good many suffered tremendous losses." He paused to see if they were following him.

Assured of both ladies' undivided attention, he continued, "It wasn't, I regret to say, any astute move on Stuart's part that saved him. He was, as I understand it, on a . . . a drinking spree with two of his cronies. I doubt that he even knew of the battle until afterwards. In fact, I am not even certain that he knew he owned any stock, or I fancy it would have been sold off along with everything else. Apparently the certificates were lost long ago, and it was only Eversleigh's remembrance of Cyrus's investment that brought it all to light. Lord Eversleigh took it upon himself to write to London and enquire about the stock on your behalf. The happy result is that you now own the stock, and it has tripled in value since Cyrus first bought in. The interest alone will provide you with a tidy income. The new certificates are being issued in your name, and if you should like, I will hold them for you in a safe place."

"Considering that they were lost once, I think that a wise idea," Hester told him. "I cannot imagine anyone being so careless, although nothing that Stuart did should surprise me any longer. So, I have Lord Eversleigh to thank for my good fortune?" The thought disconcerted her, and occupied her mind to the exclusion of all else. If he was so desperate to buy Silverdale, why did he go to so much trouble on her behalf?

A decidedly cheerful Mrs. Mulliken came in to clear the table, and she told Hester, "Ben's waiting in the kitchen, miss, and would like a word with you, when you have the time."

"I'll come now, thank you," Hester replied, and excused herself. Rundle fingered his napkin nervously, aware that Becky was watching him. As soon as the door closed behind Hester, she turned to him.

"Perhaps you will be so good as to explain to me just how Cyrus Martingale came to lose those stock certificates? If Hester didn't have her head in the clouds, she'd be asking you, too. I am undoubtedly ignorant of the ways of business, but I would have thought that as his man of business, you would have had those certificates in your possession, along with his other papers."

"Just so. I've been wondering about that myself, and I cannot think how it came about," he told her evasively.

"And another thing—I confess I know very little about the Funds and investments and such, but I find it difficult to credit that someone could simply write a letter and have lost certificates restored."

"Well, doubtless if you or I attempted to do so, we'd be mired in endless correspondence. But Lord Eversleigh is a powerful man, and there are those who would do whatever they could to oblige him."

"I see. Obviously you are among their number." He started to interrupt, but she held up her hand. "Please don't say anything more. You are fortunate that Hester trusts you so implicitly that it doesn't occur to her to question you. It all sounds rather plausible, Oliver, but I know that there is much you are not telling me, and it distresses me that you trust me so little. Now, if you'll excuse me..."

"Becky!" he implored her, and although the woebegone look he wore touched her heart, she told him curtly, "I'm sorry, Oliver, but until you feel you can trust me with the truth, there can be little for us to say to each other."

She crossed to the door and almost collided with Hester, who was hurrying into the room, anxious to relate her news.

"Becky! There is an inn called The Ram's Head. At least, we think so. Ben was talking to Zack Hawkins—he's one of the guards that Eversleigh posted—and he seems to remember a tavern by that name in Milhurst."

CHAPTER EIGHT

HESTER, BECKY AND RUNDLE were arguing over the best way to approach The Ram's Head Inn, when Lord Eversleigh called. Conscious of the gratitude she owed him, Hester generously told him Ben's news.

He immediately, and in what Hester considered a rather autocratic manner, sent for Ben and questioned him closely. But there wasn't a great deal more that Ben could tell him.

"If it's the place that Zack recollects, it's a right rough house, sir. He says it looks like a den of thieves, and they don't take too kindly to strangers dropping in."

Hester's eyes were shining with excitement. It was apparent to Eversleigh that she considered this news most promising, and he wouldn't put it past her to try to visit the inn herself. He held out a hand to her. "Will you trust me to investigate this? I promise I shall ride over there on Saturday and see what I can discover."

"But, governor," Ben couldn't help interrupting, "They won't tell you a thing, if it's the den of thieves as Zack thinks."

"Ah, Ben, you underestimate the power of greed. There's little honour among thieves. For a suitable reward most of them would turn in their own mothers. I think, if we let it be known that there's a fifty-pound reward for any information about Logenberry, we shall get a few nibbles."

"That's not all you're likely to get if you go in there flashing fifty pounds about! You might not come back out," Ben warned.

"I'm disappointed you have so little faith in me," Eversleigh drawled, adjusting the ruffle on his sleeve.

Mulliken flushed, but Hester agreed with him. "It sounds much too risky, and I can't allow you to put yourself in so much danger."

"I'm deeply touched by your concern, Miss Martingale, but I assure you that I'm not such a frippery fellow as I look."

"Aye, governor," Ben agreed. "And you strips down nicely, but these coves don't fight fair."

"Thank you, Ben. I'll keep that in mind. And since you all seem to doubt my ability to handle myself, let me reassure you that I shan't go there alone. I fancy Tobias and Zachary will give me all the protection I need."

This reference to two extremely large and brutish brothers quieted Ben, but Hester demanded to know who they were. Eversleigh patiently explained that the two brothers had once been set upon in a tavern by more than a dozen men. When the brawl was over, the two brothers were the only ones left standing. Tobias had suffered a broken hand having hit a brick wall when one of his attackers had ducked, and Zack had a broken nose. But that was nothing compared to the damage they had inflicted on the others.

Hester reluctantly agreed that they sounded like adequate guards, but extracted a promise from Eversleigh that he would call at Silverdale as soon as he returned.

He laughed at her fears, but agreed, and once that was settled, retired to the library with Rundle. Becky excused herself from joining them on the grounds that she had letters to write. Hester stared after her retreating form, wondering what was amiss. Rundle, with mournful eyes, watched her leave the room. Shoulders sagging in dejection, he woodenly followed Eversleigh to the library.

Once they were alone, Eversleigh confronted him. "Out with it, old friend, what's troubling you?"

"It's Becky, Charles. She knows I've not been entirely truthful with her and taxed me with it. She feels I don't trust her and refuses to have anything more to do with me."

"Sharp as a tack, our Becky is. I was afraid we wouldn't be able to fool her. Hester doesn't suspect anything, does she?"

"No, I don't think so. Though she might, if she takes the time to think it through. Right now she's too excited, and her mind's diverted with the idea of The Ram's Head."

"Do you think Becky will tell her of her suspicions? If Hester learned the truth, I don't think there's any chance of keeping her here."

Rundle sadly agreed. "But I doubt that Becky will say anything, at least not for some time. Even though she knows I've not been honest with her, she still seems to trust me a little."

"Trusts you! What an understatement. The woman dotes on you, Oliver, and I hope that when we see our way clear of this, you mean to put your luck to the touch."

The older man brightened. "I did think she seemed partial to my company. I only hope she'll forgive my duplicity when she learns the truth."

While the gentlemen were discussing her, Hester was busy penning invitations to Lord Petersham and Lord Mansfield. She had originally intended to write them each a brief note informing them of her decision not to sell Silverdale. Then it had occurred to her that it might be interesting, possibly even helpful, to observe their reactions when they heard her news. So instead, she invited each of them for tea the next day.

If anyone had questioned her, she would have confessed the worst crime she could imagine Lord Petersham guilty of would be dealing with free traders and buying contraband rum. As for Lord Mansfield, much as she would have liked to cast him as the villain, she really thought him too fat to bestir himself to any great degree. So she could not see any harm in her little tea party.

All the same, she had not intended to mention it to Lord Eversleigh. And would not have, if an awkward silence had not occurred when they were having tea that afternoon. Neither Becky nor Rundle seemed inclined to speak, and Eversleigh simply sat there like a great stone statue. Hester tried to fill the void.

"It will seem strange not having you gentlemen here for tea tomorrow, but we won't be without company. I've invited Lord Petersham and Lord Mansfield to join us. I thought I'd tell them both, personally, that Silverdale is no longer for sale."

"Hester, do you think that's wise?" Becky asked with concern.

"Of all the hare-brained ideas!" Eversleigh said at the same time.

"I beg your pardon..." Hester began, flaring up at once.

Becky's hand restrained her. "Dear, don't you see? As long as our Lord X thought he might obtain the house through a legitimate sale, we were fairly safe. If it becomes known that you don't intend to sell, he'll be forced to try other measures."

In truth, Hester had not considered this aspect, although she would not own it, not before Eversleigh. She replied defensively, "And none of you think the news won't be spread across the county within a day or two? Everyone is sure to know it soon, what with Mrs. Mulliken hiring that girl from the village. You may say what you will, but I prefer to see their reactions when they learn I'm staying here."

"Then I shall not deprive you of my reaction also. If you have no objections, I shall join your tea party."

Hester could think of several objections, but Becky was already effusively assuring Eversleigh that they would be glad of his company.

He thanked her civilly and, after taking a brief leave of Rundle, bowed stiffly to the ladies and left in a manner that could only be termed a huff.

"Well! Of all the overbearing, autocratic, impossible..."

"Miss Hester, pray don't be vexed with Eversleigh. He spoke in anger, and without thought, I admit, but only out of concern for your safety," Rundle said.

"If that's how he expresses his concern, I suppose I can only be thankful that he doesn't like me," she retorted, glaring at the door.

"Oh, Hester! How can you say such a thing when Lord Eversleigh has been so kind to us?"

"I assure you, Miss Hester, that you are mistaken. Lord Eversleigh holds you in the highest esteem. Indeed, he confided in me that he has a great deal of admiration for you."

Hester stared at the solicitor incredulously, but he appeared to be perfectly sincere. She stood, flustered and unable to think of anything to say. With a mumbled apology, she excused herself.

THE SITUATION was not much improved the next morning, although both Becky and Hester came down to see Rundle off. Hester thanked him warmly for all his work on her behalf, and repeated her invitation for him to visit during the summer, before leaving him with Becky.

That lady took a more formal leave of him, with the result that Rundle had more the mien of a man on his way to an execution than to London. She relented at the last moment, and gave him her hand. "I'll see you to your carriage, Oliver. Perhaps we shall meet again when you are... when you have more inclination to trust me."

His eyes lit up with hope, and he averred fervently, "It was never a question of not trusting *you*, Becky. Please believe me. It is only that I am pledged—"

"Yes, I know. You're pledged to secrecy, and well I can guess to whom. Never mind that now. I wish you a pleasant and safe journey, and if you would care to, you might write us a line to let us know of your safe arrival," she said, stepping back. The postilion had loaded his valise and stood waiting with the carriage door held open.

"Thank you for understanding, Becky. I promise you won't have reason to regret it." And with a jaunty wave, he entered the carriage. Becky watched it roll down the drive, a half smile on her lips as Oliver craned his neck for a last look at her.

She returned to the house to find Hester still in the hall. "I'm glad you were kind to him, Becky. He has been looking rather crushed the past day or two. Poor lamb."

"Humph. If I were a young lady expecting several gentlemen to tea, I'm sure I would find ample to do without wasting time standing about and spying on my elders," Becky told her sternly, but there was a twinkle in her eyes, and her lips twitched. She even hummed a little tune as she swept down the hall.

Hester, feeling unaccountably better, at once set to preparing for her tea. The drawing room was cleaned and polished, the French doors set partially open to catch the breeze. Fresh flowers filled the vases, and the enticing aroma of newly baked pies and cakes filled the hall. Everything was in readiness when the knocker sounded at four.

Lord Petersham was the first to arrive, and Hester directed him to a comfortable chair. He passed a pleasant few minutes in idle conversation with her and Becky before Eversleigh was shown in. Hester felt her colour rise as she greeted him, and recalled Rundle's words. But there was nothing in Eversleigh's manner to betray either the annoyance he had felt at their last meeting, or any of the admiration he was supposed to feel for his hostess. He spoke to her politely enough before turning to engage Petersham in conversation about some sort of new irrigation system.

Much admiration, indeed, Hester thought ruefully as she poured his tea. The door opened again, and Alice announced Miss Derringham and Mr. Percival Mansfield. The ladies exchanged cool greetings, and while Hermione strolled over to speak to Eversleigh, Mansfield explained, "I hope you don't object to my standing in for my father, Miss Martingale. He's feeling out of sorts and begged me to act as his deputy."

"Not at all," Hester demurred.

"And Hermione insisted I bring her when she learned I was coming to Silverdale."

"I am, of course, delighted to see her again," Hester said, handing him his tea, and shooting a dark glance at Hermione. Eversleigh was lounging in his favourite position, with one arm resting on the mantel of the fireplace. Hermione stood close to his side, and as Hester watched, she whispered something softly to him that caused him to laugh aloud. Hester decided it was time to make her announcement. She stood and asked for their attention.

"I'm sure you are all wondering why I invited you here this afternoon. As you know, there was considerable doubt that Stuart's estate would leave me in a financially secure position, and several of you, out of kindness I'm sure, made me an offer to purchase Silverdale. I wanted to tell you personally that the estate has finally been settled, and it is not necessary that I sell after all. In other words, my dear friends, Becky and I will be remaining at Silverdale."

"Why, this is wonderful news," Petersham said, crossing to her side. "You, and Miss Becky, are a welcome addition to our neighbourhood. My lady will be pleased to hear you mean to stay."

Percy carefully set down his cup and adjusted his collar. "I, too, am delighted by your news, Miss Martingale, but I confess I'm somewhat surprised. I had not thought Stuart's estate sufficient to allow you to continue on here."

Eversleigh spoke before Hester could reply. "Some stock came to light that Stuart apparently forgot he owned. Miss Martingale shall be able to live quite comfortably on the interest."

"I see. You seem to know quite a bit about it, Eversleigh."

"Oh, he's been here every day for weeks helping the solicitor go through Stuart's papers," Hermione contributed sweetly.

Hester returned to her seat and poured a fresh cup of tea. She spoke quietly to Petersham. "I am sorry you will have to find another house for your sister now."

"Don't give it a thought. She finally landed, er, she became engaged a few days back. I meant to let you know, but the family's been in an uproar ever since."

Hester laughed at his expression, but couldn't help wondering if his sister's engagement was really sudden, or if she had only been an excuse to offer for the house. He appeared totally unconcerned with her news, and she didn't know him well enough to judge if he was sincere.

She turned her attention to Percy, who was addressing Lord Eversleigh. "You must be devastated by this news. I know how you coveted Silverdale."

"No, I only wanted it restored, Percy. Miss Martingale will take excellent care of it, I'm sure."

"Undoubtedly, unless..." Percy let his words trail off.

"Unless?" Eversleigh prompted.

"I was only thinking of how unsettled Stuart left his affairs. You know, the intruders and the incident with the dog... I do hope Miss Martingale does not encounter any further difficulties."

Petersham was listening now with close attention, and spoke up, "Are you referring to those rumours about Stuart engaging in blackmail? I never did put any stock in that. It's all nonsense."

"I wish I could be so sure," Eversleigh said. "We found an interesting note among Stuart's papers. A clue of sorts. I'm following it up tomorrow."

Hester's cup clinked against the table as she set it down abruptly, aghast at what Eversleigh was revealing.

Percy was all ears. "What kind of note? Evidence of blackmail?"

"Perhaps. It's too soon to say. I'll know more after I visit a little inn known as The Ram's Head. I go there tomorrow."

"How fascinating, Eversleigh. You must keep me apprised, but now I must get back to Father. The old boy's not feeling at all the thing, and he gets on the fret if I'm not there to pander to him. Hermione, my dear, are you ready?"

Hermione left with him, reluctantly, and Lord Petersham took his leave a few minutes later. Hester could barely contain her wrath until he had left the room. She took a deep breath and tried to speak calmly. "Lord Eversleigh, I believe it was only yesterday that you referred to me as 'hare-brained' for merely telling those two gentlemen that I would not be selling this house. Perhaps you would care to explain why you now choose to reveal to those same gentlemen our only real clue? I find it difficult to credit—"

"Hester, if you will only listen—"

"That a gentleman of your supposed intelligence could fail to comprehend—"

Becky came into the room exclaiming, "Goodness! I can hear your voices in the hall, and no doubt so can everyone else in the neighbourhood."

Hester took a turn about the room, twisting her handkerchief in her agitation. "I am sorry, Becky. I was only trying to discover what possessed Lord Eversleigh to tell the others about the inn."

Eversleigh had resumed his pose by the fireplace and replied languidly, "You would discover a great deal more if you would allow me an opportunity to speak. I was attempting to explain to you that I was merely baiting a trap."

"A trap? Do you mean—"

"Precisely. If any of the persons here today are involved, mention of The Ram's Head must surely stir them to some sort of action. I didn't think you were able to discern any evidence of guilt by watching their reactions to your news."

"No," she admitted absently, considering this new idea, "but might not this put you in danger?"

"Hardly. You did notice that I neglected to mention that Zack and Tobias would accompany me. I fancy they are more than a match for Mansfield, or even Petersham. And they can certainly handle our friend Derringham."

"Lord Derringham? Do you think Hermione will tell her father what was said?"

"If you knew her better, you'd not cherish any doubts on that head." He grinned. "That woman has a tongue that runs on greased wheels. She'll entertain her father tonight at dinner by repeating every word and gesture of ours."

"How disparagingly you speak of her, my lord, and yet you seem much attracted to her company," Hester replied, momentarily diverted.

"I am," he owned. "Hermione is a beautiful woman, and on occasion, even her gossip can be highly amusing."

"Children! Really, this is a most improper conversation," Becky chided. "And not at all to the purpose. Tell me, Lord Eversleigh, do you truly suspect Derringham?"

"No, no more than Petersham, or Mansfield, but none of them can be ruled out."

"It must be one of the three," Hester mused. "But Derringham did not make an offer to buy the house."

"Perhaps he felt it would do no good," Eversleigh said, setting down his cup and preparing to take his leave. He cast an amused look at Hester. "You said *three*. Does that mean I am no longer on your list of suspects?"

Hester flushed, and Becky was quick to declaim, "Why, what a jokester you are to suggest such a thing!"

He smiled at Becky, while his eyes remained steadfastly on Hester, and he awaited her answer. Flustered, she turned away, and busied herself with the tea tray. She didn't see the hurt look that flashed across his features. Becky did, and tried to make amends, assuring him that he was held in the highest regard, and they were both deeply indebted to him for his many acts of kindness.

"Thank you, Miss Becky, you have a generous heart. Now, I'd best see what mischief my brothers have contrived in my absence."

Hester stood mutely while Becky showed him out. He'd done it again. Caught her off balance and made her as awkward as any schoolroom miss. Drat the man.

Becky returned to find Hester subjecting the teacups to rather harsh treatment, roughly banging them down on the tray. She rescued the set before any damage was done, and then treated Hester to a pithy lecture on the sin of ingratitude.

The young woman had nothing to say in her defence, and Becky, seeing her remorsefulness, relented. "Well, what's done is done. I only pray that Lord Eversleigh comes to no harm tomorrow."

Hester's head jerked up. "Surely his guards will protect him? You don't truly think he stands in any danger, do you?"

"Lord, child, if our suspicions are correct, he's practically invited the villain to try to stop him. He's either a very courageous man or a very foolhardy one."

The colour slowly drained from Hester's face. Her vivid imagination immediately conjured up an image of Eversleigh lying by the roadside, his life's blood draining from him. She sat down abruptly. "I shall never forgive myself if anything happens to him."

"There now, don't go enacting a Cheltenham tragedy where there's none. I won't say he don't stand in danger, but I fancy he's one as is able to take care of himself. Like as not, he'll be here late tomorrow, safe and sound. And being a man, will likely have enjoyed the adventure hugely."

WHILE EVERSLEIGH did not doubt his ability to face any man on equal footing, he knew he wasn't safe from an ambush. He'd left word for Zack and Toby to call at the manor house that evening, and when they arrived, he took them into the library. He wanted to be certain they understood the danger they might be facing.

Zack had heard of The Ram's Head, and wasn't bashful at saying how it was no place for his lordship to be visiting.

"I'm afraid I've little choice in the matter," Eversleigh replied. "My only hope of finding out what really happened to Martingale lies in that inn."

"Like that, is it, governor? Well, you can count us in," Zack told him, and Toby nodded in agreement.

"Thank you, but I want you both to understand that a possible brawl is not the worst of it." He paused and lit his cigar, blowing a cloud of smoke before continuing. "You see, a number of people know that I plan to make this little trip tomorrow, and I have every reason to believe that one of them will try to prevent me."

"Lawks, governor! If I'd known it was to be that kind of game, I'd have brought along my pea-shooter."

"I have arms enough for us all, but ... unless it's absolutely necessary, I don't wish our assailant to be killed."

Zack shook his head despairingly. "I ain't no fine gentleman like you, and I don't always ken the way the quality behaves. But when a cove takes and sets up to ambush you..." He shrugged.

"Under other circumstances, Zack, I'd agree. This time, however, I hope to catch the wretch, and put a few home questions to him—which would be extremely difficult were he dead."

It took moments, but Toby's face lit up as he finally comprehended what Eversleigh meant. Zack was already shaking hands and saying as how they'd do their best.

"Now, Martha will show you the way to your rooms. I want you here so we can get an early start in the morning. We leave at first light," he warned.

Eversleigh opened the oak door and called for Martha. None of them saw the young boy who peered over the window-sill at the far end of the room. He ducked back down quickly, and crawled along the terrace until he reached the French doors giving off the drawing room.

Harry had known something was afoot when Zack and Toby were sent for. When he had questioned Charlie, as was his custom, he had met with a terse command to see to his studies. Understandably indignant at being consigned to the schoolroom, Harry had bided his time.

Not long after dinner he had strategically retired to his room. As soon as he judged it safe, he crept down the servants' stairwell at the rear of the house. Carefully unlatching the door at the end of the long hall, he slipped out and was soon hidden among the shrubbery beneath an open library window.

His brother's mention of The Ram's Head was the first Harry had heard of that clue, and he thought it dastardly of Charlie to keep it to himself. His eyes grew large at the mention of a possible ambush and trap, and he almost gave himself away in his excitement. When he heard Charles start to show the brothers out, he chanced a look over the sill. The men were still at the door of the hall, and he quickly ducked out of sight.

Harry crawled along the terrace to the drawing room, his heart beating fast. Edging through the room as quietly as possible, he reached the hall and raced up the stairs to his room. Out of breath and full of excitement, he began to think out a plan of action. Regretfully, he decided he could not include Jack. His brother was still recovering, and if events turned dangerous, Jack might not be able to ride swiftly enough. He grinned ruefully. When Jack found out about this, he'd be mad as fire at being left out. But, Harry assured himself, he, at least, had a good reason for not including his younger brother.

Richard was enlisted to wake him early. Harry told him he'd promised to go over to Miss Hester's and give Ben a hand in the stables. Richard, who, as usual, had his head in a book, didn't question him, and Harry returned to his room well satisfied. He was not normally an early riser, and he deemed it wise to retire early and get a good night's rest.

He was noticeably less enthusiastic the next morning when Richard woke him. A glance out the window showed the sun had not yet risen, and he regarded his bed with longing. He looked outside again and saw Toby trudging across the drive. That was enough to restore his sense of purpose, and Harry scrambled into his clothes. He furtively watched from the window until he saw Charlie's Town carriage roll down the drive. Toby was up on the box, and he assumed Charlie and Zack must be hidden within.

Harry rushed from the room and down the stairs, making a swift stop in the gun room. He carefully re-

moved the long rifle Charlie had given him when he'd begun to hunt the year before. He dared not risk stopping in
the kitchen for a bite, although a tantalizing aroma of
fresh-baked bread was drifting into the hall as he slipped
out the side door.

Cloud pranced about nervously as he saddled her. The
little mare sensed his excitement and nudged him several
times. "Patience, old girl, we'll soon be off." Harry knew
he dared not follow too closely, and yet he had to keep the
carriage in sight since he didn't know the direction. He
kept well to the side of the road, and far enough back so
he could see the carriage but couldn't be recognized. If
they took the Pike Road, he'd have to chance getting
closer or likely end up following the wrong carriage.

He heaved a sigh of relief when the carriage turned left
at the crossroads. At least they weren't taking the Pike.
Harry pulled Cloud up, dropping back a bit and loping
along at an easy pace. They covered several miles, and although he was keeping a sharp eye on the woods bound-
ing the road, there wasn't any sight or sound of likely
trouble. The excitement of the chase slowly gave way to
boredom as the hours passed, and Harry's stomach began to make uncomfortable rumbling noises, reminding
him that he'd not eaten.

He eyed his brother's carriage enviously, sure that
Charlie had provisions within, and tortured himself by
imagining the delicious morsels he and Zack were probably eating. The thought of food led naturally to thoughts
of drink. The sun rose higher and Harry felt he could actually taste the dust lodged in his throat. He made up his
mind to brave Charlie's wrath and join the carriage party
if they showed signs of pulling off the road for a nun-
cheon.

By the time the noon hour approached, Harry was tired and dusty. It no longer seemed like an exciting adventure and even Cloud had lost her enthusiasm. He gave the reins a light tug and nudged the mare to a faster gait. The devil with it, he thought, deciding to catch up with his brother. At least Charles would give him food and drink before ordering him home.

The carriage rounded a bend in the road, and he lost sight of it for a few minutes. Urging Cloud on, he rounded the same curve and suddenly saw two masked horsemen erupt from the copse just behind the carriage.

Tobias, up on the box, heard their hoofbeats. "Here they comes, governor—get ready!" he warned. Inside the carriage, Charles and Zack each primed a pistol and held them at the ready. Toby pulled the plunging team to a halting stop and reached for his own rifle. He let off a shot just over the head of the first rider.

The horseman was startled by the gunfire. His chestnut reared up, and he tried to steady her as he returned the fire. His shot was wide of the mark, but the coachman wasn't his target. It was the tall gentleman who'd be riding inside that he'd been ordered to set upon. He wheeled his horse, narrowly dodging a shot that came from the door of the carriage. His partner, a shorter, heavier rider, cursed. Yelling that he'd been hit, the heavier man kicked his horse and raced across the fields to the woods on the right.

Another rider was approaching fast behind them. When he, too, loosed a shot that just missed, the masked rider took to the fields after his confederate. Toby, seeing a third rider approaching with his rifle at the ready, took careful aim and fired. The bullet caught Harry in the right shoulder, causing him to drop the rifle.

"Got him!" Toby declared jubilantly, and Charles and Zack cautiously emerged from the carriage. Harry was closer now, one arm clasping his shoulder, the reins dragging.

"Don't shoot," he cried. "Charlie, it's me. I've been hit."

"Oh, God! It's Master Harry," Zack yelled, and Toby looked near to fainting. Charles said nothing, though his face paled and the tiny muscle near his eyes pulsated. He jogged forward and caught Cloud by the reins, just in time to catch Harry as he fell. The boy's tunic was drenched in blood. Charles eased him to the ground, and Harry fainted dead away.

CHAPTER NINE

BECKY WATCHED HESTER cross to the windows overlooking the drive for what was perhaps the fifth time within the last hour. After a moment, Hester dejectedly let the drapery fall and turned to catch Becky's eyes on her. "I thought I heard a carriage," she said defensively.

"If there was anything out there, you may be sure Blackie would let us know," Becky told her. They both looked at the huge dog sprawled in front of the fireplace, head resting on his paws. He seemed far too content to move if anyone did approach. But the instant Mrs. Mulliken entered the room, the great head lifted, the ears came up and his tongue came out in a drool. Blackie knew it was well past the dinner hour.

Hester, her stomach decidedly queasy, had asked the housekeeper to set dinner back an hour. The time had past, and she still had little desire to sit down to eat. Only the militant look in Mrs. Mulliken's eyes persuaded her, for she knew she would have no peace unless she agreed.

The two ladies sat down alone, and, of course, the main topic of conversation was Eversleigh's delay. "There could be any number of reasons why we haven't heard from him," Becky said. "It's even possible that Eversleigh was unable to visit the inn today. Something could've occurred on his estates to detain him."

"If that were so, surely he'd have sent us word. He promised to call here as soon as he returned. He must know how worried we would be."

"If he didn't forget his promise altogether," Becky answered tartly. "It's been my experience that gentlemen are not the most reliable of creatures. Only let word get about of a boxing match or sporting event and everything else seems to fly out of their mindless heads."

Hester found herself in the unique position of defending Eversleigh. "I cannot believe it of Eversleigh. He would not use me so badly." She laid down her spoon and faced Becky. "I fear something dreadful has occurred."

"Do you, now? I fancy there's a more rational explanation. Those three great men would not have come to harm easily. I believe it's far more likely that they lost their direction or, perhaps, a wheel off the carriage. Or one of the horses could have been lamed. I think that's much more probable—especially with those brothers along."

Hester smiled wanly and strove to appear more cheerful. Yet she toyed with her food, and Becky's sharp eyes did not miss that. She thought if Hester continued this way, she'd fret herself sick. When they returned to the drawing room, Becky sent Alice out to fetch Ben.

At Hester's look of surprise, she told her, "No sense in sitting here stewing when there's a simple enough way to learn if Eversleigh is safe or not. Ben will drive you over to the manor and you may see if there is any news. Take Alice with you. I'll wait here just in case."

Hester gave her a grateful look before running up the stairs. She could not bear to sit still any longer, waiting, imagining all sorts of horrors. At least this would give her something to do. It was only a very few minutes before they were ready to set out, and Ben, almost as anxious as his mistress, sprang the horses.

Hester didn't know what she expected; however, the sight of the manor house brilliantly lit, with candles in every window, did little to calm her. She waited impatiently for Ben to reach the centre drive, and was scrambling out of the carriage before the horses had fully stopped. Alice had to hurry to keep up with her.

Hester sounded the knocker loudly, and the door was opened abruptly by one of the housemaids. Hester wondered fleetingly where Hodges, Eversleigh's very correct butler, was. She brushed the thought aside, and to the girl's enquiry, demanded to know if Lord Eversleigh was at home.

"Yes, miss—" the girl bobbed, "—but he's frightfully busy just now."

Hester was taken aback. Fully expecting to hear that Eversleigh was away, she stared at the girl for a moment, before demanding, "Is he well? He's not hurt in any way?"

"No, miss, but—"

"Never mind," Hester said, cutting the girl off in her fury. "That was all I desired to know. You may tell his lordship that Miss Martingale called. Good evening."

The housemaid watched helplessly as Hester and Alice returned to their carriage. She had been about to tell the lady that Master Harry had been fearfully wounded, and his lordship was in the boy's room with Dr. Layton. Even Hodges was up there.

Ben saw the anger in Hester's face and hesitated to question her. Hester relieved him of the necessity. As soon as she was seated, she told him, "Drive us home at once, Ben. There is no need for us here. Eversleigh is safe at home."

"Did he go to the inn, miss?" he dared ask.

"I did not enquire," Hester replied icily. "Perhaps his lordship will feel it incumbent upon him to enlighten us tomorrow. Obviously, he did not consider our interest in the affair of sufficient import to delay him this evening."

Alice and Ben exchanged a wary look. Neither had seen Hester in such a temper before. The drive home was a silent one. Ben drew up the horses, and Hester was out, striding to the house before Alice could move. She scrambled after her mistress and opened the door in time to hear Hester, her voice raised in unchecked anger.

"You may cease worrying yourself over that wretched man, Becky. His lordship is safe at home, and from the way the house is lit, I suspect he's hosting a party. Candles in every window. To think that I—"

Becky quickly crossed the room and closed the door. "Really, Hester, you sound more like a fisher-woman than a lady of quality. When you have calmed yourself, I shall be interested to learn what occurred."

Becky's rebuke and calm voice had their effect. Hester took a deep breath and stooped to give Blackie a reassuring caress. When she had regained a measure of composure, she apologized.

"It's only that I am so furious when I think of how we sat here all afternoon and evening, apprehensive for that man's safety. And it is just as you predicted. Lord Eversleigh is safe at home, and doubtless has no memory of the promise he made me."

"Did he visit the inn at all?"

Hester shrugged. "I didn't bother to stay and enquire. As soon as the housemaid told me he was home, and well, I said good evening."

Becky looked at her sadly. "You might have given him an opportunity to explain. Perhaps there was a reason—"

"I didn't wish to intrude, Becky. As I told you, the house was brightly lit. I feel certain he is expecting a large number of guests. Even Hodges was not at his post. A young housemaid answered the door, and it was she who told me he was at home. I did make certain that he had not been harmed in any way, but more than that I would not ask. Now, if you'll excuse me, I'm rather tired."

Becky watched her leave with a feeling of foreboding. In spite of what she'd said to Hester earlier, she suspected Lord Eversleigh had a very good reason for not calling. He didn't seem to her to be the sort of gentleman who was careless of his obligations. There had to be a reason, and she only wished she knew what it was.

The reason, young Harry, was at that moment lying in his own bed. Dr. Layton had removed the bullet from his shoulder and bandaged it. There was not much more he could do for the lad, who kept passing in and out of consciousness. Harry was delirious and alternated between shouting warnings to his brother and apologizing for being such a fool. Layton didn't believe him to be aware of their presence. Both Eversleigh and Hodges had assisted him, and he motioned for the butler to remove the bloody linens and bowl of water, before turning to Eversleigh.

"Now, Charles, I prescribe a stiff brandy for the two of us, and you may tell me how this came about."

Eversleigh stood by Harry's side, a hand pressed anxiously over the boy's brow. His brother had lost an alarming amount of blood before they had got him home, and he silently prayed for his recovery. The doctor stepped to his side and laid a comforting arm on his shoulders.

"Let us have that drink. There's nothing more we can do here, and Harry will sleep for some time. But I promise you, he's out of danger. The wound looks a great deal worse than it is."

Charles reluctantly agreed, but had his valet come in to watch over Harry, with orders to send for him at once, should the boy wake.

The men settled in the library, and Charles poured two liberal drinks before beginning his tale. Their glasses were almost empty when he concluded, "Poor Harry came galloping up, rifle at the ready, bent on rescuing me. Tobias mistook him for one of the highwaymen and put a bullet in his shoulder. You know the rest."

"Aye and I pity Tobias. I don't believe I've ever seen the big fellow look so forlorn. Took it hard. I had to give him a dose of laudanum to calm him down. He should sleep the night through now, but where's that brother of his?"

"Zack?" Charles held the brandy up and motioned for his friend's glass. "He agreed that one of us should still pay The Ram's Head a call."

"Alone? Do you think that's wise?"

"No, but I have an extreme dislike of being ambushed, and Zack seems to share my aversion. Someone went to extraordinary lengths to prevent us from visiting that inn, and we don't intend he should be successful."

Layton shook his head. "I trust you know what you're doing, Charles. This game you're playing grows dangerous. Don't misunderstand me. It's not you or Zack that I worry about, but Hester Martingale."

"I give you my word, Josiah, her safety is—Oh, Lord! I completely forgot. I was supposed to call at Silverdale as soon as I returned. She must be thinking I'm dead or worse, unless..." He crossed the room while Layton watched in open-mouthed puzzlement.

Before Eversleigh could open the door, Hodges entered. "Beggin' your pardon, my lord, but one of the housemaids has informed me that Miss Martingale called while we were abovestairs with Master Harry."

"Yes, I rather thought she might have. Why wasn't I told?" Eversleigh's voice was deadly calm as he reseated himself.

Hodges fastened his eyes on the wall and replied in measured tones, "Miss Martingale did not wish to remain, sir. The girl says Miss Martingale enquired if you were at home, and then if you were well. As soon as she learned you were safe, Miss Martingale took her leave."

"And she left no message for me?"

"No, sir. Except to say that she had called."

"I see. Do you know if the maid happened to mention that Harry had been severely wounded?"

"No, sir. Marie says she started to, but the lady was in a frightful hurry and didn't give her the chance."

"Very well, Hodges. That's all, thank you." Charles turned to his friend. Layton was trying, unsuccessfully, to smother a laugh. "I'm glad you find this so amusing, Josiah. Hester will have my head for breakfast."

"And justly so. Allowing that sweet young lady to worry over you all evening. I wonder if it's too late to pay her a call? I'd give a pony to be in the drawing room with Miss Martingale and Miss Becky this moment. It would be so refreshing to hear you categorized as the inconsiderate, thoughtless cad you are. I do grow tired of seeing young ladies toady to you. Not to mention their mamas."

"Then perhaps you'd care to bear me company when I call in the morning to make amends?"

"No," Layton told him regretfully, rising from his comfortable chair. "I have no doubt you'll bring them round, and then I'd be embarrassed to stay and listen to their shameless flattery and offers of tea and sympathy."

"What a notion you have of me. I only wish you might be right. At times, I think Hester holds me in dislike. It's only occasionally that she relents enough to allow me to perform some trifling service for her."

"You have only to tell her of Harry's mishap to win instant forgiveness. Speaking of the lad, I want another look at him before I take my leave. And I'll look in again in the morning."

DR. LAYTON WAS ONLY half right in his prophecy. When Lord Eversleigh called at Silverdale the next morning, Alice informed him that Miss Martingale was indisposed, and Miss Becky had driven into the village with Ben. Charles stood idly in the hall, deliberating, while Alice privately thought her mistress run mad to turn away such an elegant gentleman. Eversleigh was looking particularly handsome in close-fitting riding attire and boots. His blond hair was unpowdered and fell in natural curls, while his green eyes held a warm smile. Alice could not stop herself. She blurted out impulsively, "Miss Hester thought some fresh air might help her headache. She's cutting flowers in the garden," she added, nodding towards the rear of the house.

Eversleigh blessed her for a kind and generous lass, which brought the colour up in her cheeks. "Get on with ye, do," she told him merrily, and he didn't wait for further urging.

Charles rounded the house and spied Hester at the far end of the garden. He paused for a minute, watching her and thinking how charming she looked. Hester was wearing a green-and-white-striped gown of muslin. The chip straw hat she wore to protect her complexion went well with the woven basket she carried on her arm. Hester added another rose to her collection and then, as though she felt his eyes on her, looked up.

"Good morning, Miss Martingale," Charles called, advancing. "I have important news for you."

"I see you number trespassing among your other faults, sir. I left instructions that I was indisposed and could not receive visitors."

He admired the way her chin lifted whenever she was vexed. "Yes, Alice told me you had the headache, but I thought my news must act as a restorative. I knew you would want to hear about The Ram's Head."

"You mistake the matter, sir. Last evening I wished to hear of the inn. Today I have no interest in the matter."

"I think your interest might return when I tell you that I was set upon by highwaymen yesterday." He watched as her head came up, and he added gravely, "I would have kept my promise to call had not Harry been shot."

"Harry?" The colour drained from her face, and the basket dropped unheeded to the ground. Charles stepped closer, fearful she might faint, and hastened to add, "Wounded. In the shoulder. Let us sit down and I'll tell you what occurred."

Hester allowed him to lead her to a stone bench conveniently situated in the centre of the gardens. She listened to him with rapt attention, only remotely aware of the impropriety of sitting with him unchaperoned, her hand still clasped in his. Nor did she see Alice watching approvingly from an upper chamber window.

When Eversleigh had finished his tale, Hester responded as Dr. Layton had foretold, with sympathy—but it was all for Harry. "The poor boy. I must go and see him this afternoon." She suddenly became aware of the warmth of Eversleigh's hands on hers, and hastily withdrew her own as she made to rise.

"Don't run away just yet. You haven't heard everything. While Toby and I struggled to get Harry home, Zack rode on to the inn."

"Did he find Logenberry?" she asked anxiously.

"No, but someone seemed to recall a man of that name. And Zack let it be known that a handsome reward will be paid for any information leading to him. And also that if this Logenberry will talk with me, he'll be well paid for his trouble."

Hester considered this, and then found a flaw in his plan. "If this...this person is guilty of some heinous misdeed, then surely he will not come forward. He must fear he'd be taken up. Especially now, with Harry being wounded."

"He couldn't have anything to do with the attack on us yesterday. There was too little time to arrange it. My guess is Logenberry is just a pawn. A pawn used by our Lord X. It's his master who's the real criminal, and I don't intend he should escape."

"I see your point, but still...well, never mind. Tell me instead how Harry does." They passed a pleasant half hour before finally strolling back to the house, seemingly on the best of terms. Becky had returned, and Eversleigh had to retell his story for her benefit. She listened without interruption, and only remarked tersely that she hoped the boys would not dream up any more ways to help Eversleigh.

Eversleigh nodded. "I pray not, but I shall be more careful. At least they won't be able to get into much mischief for a while, with only one good pair of arms between them."

"Humph. I'd not wager against it," Becky warned. "If they need help, likely they'd drag little Jenny into it."

"Oh, Becky, don't even think such a thing," Hester cried. She turned impulsively to Eversleigh. "Perhaps Jenny could come and stay with us for a few days? Not that I think the boys would do anything to endanger her, but you'll have your hands full with them, and she might feel a little neglected."

"An excellent notion," Charles agreed readily, quick to see the advantage of having his younger sister installed at Silverdale. "We'll arrange it when you visit this afternoon." He left the ladies to their preparations, and set off on his errands in a much happier frame of mind.

It was late in the afternoon when the ladies finally arrived at Eversleigh Manor. Both ladies were distressed anew to find Harry looking so wan. He had regained consciousness early in the morning, but was still feeling very weak, and he tired easily. Dr. Layton had agreed he could have visitors, but only for a few minutes at a time. Jack sat on the foot of the bed, regarding his brother as something of a hero. Not even Charlie had suffered a bullet wound.

Hester laughed aloud at that, but not unkindly. She left Becky with the boys and went off to find Jennifer. The little girl was in her room, and as Hester tapped on the door, she could hear the child talking softly to Mademoiselle DuBarry. The grave little voice bade her enter, but as soon as Jenny saw who it was, she jumped up to greet her warmly.

"I've missed you, Jenny. It seems quite a long time since you paid me a visit."

Jenny nodded. "Mademoiselle and I *wanted* to come to see you, but Charlie won't allow me to go alone, and everyone has been too busy to go with me. Harry got shot, did you know?"

"Yes, your brother told me. Becky is visiting him now."

"Everybody makes such a fuss over him, but Mademoiselle and I don't care. We have each other for company." She straightened her doll's hat and pretended to be unconcerned.

"Becky and I thought you and Mademoiselle might be a little lonely. How would you like to come and stay with me for a few days?"

"Oh, Miss Hester, may I? Did Charlie say I could? What about Miss Fontaine?" Jenny was up and dancing about the room in her excitement.

"Both your brother and Miss Fontaine have agreed. She's going to send a maid up to pack some of your things, and then you can go back with me this afternoon."

"And Mademoiselle, too?"

"Of course. Now, let's go join your brother for tea and give your maid a chance to pack."

Jenny slipped her hand in Hester's as they left the room. Charles was waiting for them in the yellow drawing room, and a lovely tea had been laid. Becky, with Jack in tow, entered directly behind them, and Jenny immediately taunted him, "I'm going to stay with Miss Hester for a week—maybe longer!" Hester's eyes met Charles's and they shared a smile.

Eversleigh directed Hester to a sofa and asked her to pour the tea for them. They presented a charming picture. Hester sat on the Chippendale sofa with Jenny close beside her and Mademoiselle nestled in the corner. Becky occupied one of the high-backed chairs and Jack had a footstool near her. Charles, as was his custom, remained standing by the fireplace. They were a handsome group, and to the unbiased eye would have looked the ideal of a happy family.

Hermione Derringham, however, was not unbiased. Hodges announced her arrival, and she entered on her father's arm, taking in the cosy scene at a glance. The hateful look she directed at Hester and Jenny was quickly veiled as Charles crossed the room to greet her and Lord Derringham.

"This is an unexpected pleasure," he said politely, leading her to the sofa opposite Hester.

"I do hope we're not intruding, but I had to come when I heard about Harry being shot," Hermione returned, arranging the skirts of her elegant walking dress.

"Aye," Derringham said with a nod. "She wouldn't give me a minute's peace until I agreed to drive her over here. How's the lad doing?"

"Much better, thank you, although he won't have the use of his arm for some time," Charles said, handing Lord Derringham a glass of sherry, assuming, correctly, that he'd prefer it to tea.

Hermione seemed to make an effort to be gracious as she accepted a cup from Hester's hands, though it was evident she deeply resented another woman acting as hostess for Charles. She looked up at him and, laughing a little, said, "I think you must own I was right, Charles."

"In what regard, Hermione?"

"Why, school, of course, for those boisterous brothers of yours. If they had been in a proper school, they wouldn't be turning your house upside down, breaking their bones and getting themselves shot."

Lord Derringham added his support, "Hermione's right, Eversleigh. Boys need the discipline of a good school. Does them a world of good. Why, look at you. You went away to school, and it did not hurt you any."

"Not in a physical sense, perhaps, but I can still remember how dreadfully lonely I was. There's time enough for them to attend school when they're older."

"Really, Charles," Hermione chided, "you're too ridiculously sentimental. Anyone would think you were their father instead of an elder brother. Don't you agree, Miss Martingale?"

"I believe the boys' schooling is a matter which only Lord Eversleigh can decide."

And Becky, in sweet innocence, asked, "Did you go away to school, Miss Derringham?"

"Yes, of course. *And* Miss Montague's Finishing School, as well." She stared at Jenny. "It's so important for a young girl to learn proper deportment. Why, I was already at school when I was Jennifer's age."

Tears welled up in Jenny's eyes, and with a sobbed, "Excuse me, please," she ran from the room.

"There! That's exactly what I mean. The child is much too attached to you, Charles. It's not healthy."

Hester stood up before he could reply. "If you will allow me, my lord, I'll go after her." At a nod from Charles, she left the room. Becky rose as well and murmured, "I'll just see how the maid is doing with the packing. So nice to see you again, Miss Derringham, Lord Derringham."

Eversleigh barely held his temper in check, and one glance at his countenance turned Hermione sulky. Her father looked from one to the other, and hastily manufactured an excuse to visit the stables. His exit was barely noticed.

Hermione remained seated and played with the gilt-edged fan she carried. Charles poured himself a drink before sitting down opposite her. Taking a deep breath, he asked calmly, ''My dear Hermione, was that really nec essary?''

''I'm afraid I don't take your meaning, Charles.''

''Then allow me to clarify matters. I will *not* send the children away to school, and particularly not Jenny. She suffered terribly when our parents died. I believe she fears she'll lose me, too—''

''But Charles,'' she interrupted, ''that's just my point. She's overly attached to you. And as for the boys, they are certainly old enough. Judging from this latest exploit, they surely can use the discipline.''

''The boys mind me well enough. Harry didn't disobey me. Indeed, he thought he was riding to my rescue.''

''Yes, I heard all about it. You're involved in all this nonsense about Stuart's death. And that's another matter I wish to discuss with you. I cannot comprehend why you feel obligated to devote so much attention to that little governess.'' She gave a girlish laugh. ''I must warn you, dear Charles, you're likely to turn her head with all this attention.''

''That is highly unlikely. Miss Martingale is a remarkable lady. If she should ever hold me in esteem, I would be flattered.''

''Then you are blind!'' The fan snapped against her hand. ''Can't you see how she's setting her cap for you— worming her way into your graces by playing up to those ridiculous children? Any fool can see—''

''Then I must be a very great fool. I think this conversation has gone on long enough. I may value your friendship, Hermione, but it does not give you licence to dictate my choice of other friends.''

''Friendship? Is that what you call it now? When we've practically been betrothed since the cradle?'' A handkerchief appeared, and she applied it delicately to her eyes.

In a gentler tone, he told her, "I'm sorry, Hermione, but it *is* only friendship. I've never given you cause to suppose that it was more."

"How can you say so? Before *she* came, we rode together every day. I always acted as your hostess. The attention you bestowed on me was such that—"

"Come now, Hermione. That was only while you amused yourself rusticating. What of the liaisons you formed in Paris? Marchand? Lord Sylvan? Did you think I didn't know?"

That was precisely what she had thought. She took further recourse to her handkerchief. Charles moved to place a comforting arm across her shoulders. Hermione, seeing her father approach the terrace doors beyond Eversleigh, tried to turn his gesture into an embrace. Charles side-stepped and neatly eluded her, and Lord Derringham, seeing the fury in his daughter's eyes, almost retreated.

Charles halted him. "Ah, sir, Hermione was just wondering where you were. She is ready to take her leave."

Hermione glared at him and, ignoring her father, stalked from the room. The two men exchanged rueful glances, and a glimmer of understanding was in the old lord's eyes as they shook hands.

Becky came in directly after and enquired of Eversleigh, "Is anything amiss? Miss Derringham nearly ran me down in the hall."

"No," Charles said with a grin, looking for all the world like a little boy up to mischief. "Not at all. In fact, all's right with the world."

Becky stared at him, and he was just saved from her questioning by Hester's entrance with Jenny. It was apparent the child had been crying; her blue eyes were rimmed with red. Still, she gave him a tremulous smile.

"Miss Hester says if it's fair weather tomorrow, we may have a picnic."

"Well, you're a very lucky young lady," he said, stooping and wiping away the last vestige of tears. With a lopsided grin, he looked up at Hester. "Wish *I* were going on a picnic."

"You can come, too, Charlie," Jenny offered generously. "Can't he, Miss Hester?"

"Can I?" he asked, standing up.

"May I," Hester corrected and laughed. "Of course you may, but it will be a very tame party."

"I think I've had enough excitement for a few days," he told her as he escorted them out to the gig. He handed up Jenny's valise, and then, picking up the little girl in his arms, kissed her soundly. Two skinny arms stole around his neck, and Jenny whispered into his collar, "I love you, Charlie."

He returned the hug and whispered into her ear. Jenny's smile widened, and the blue eyes fairly danced.

"What did your brother say to you?" Hester asked curiously, when they were under way.

"I can't tell you. It's a secret. Charlie said I mustn't tell anyone. Not even Mademoiselle."

CHAPTER TEN

HESTER STIRRED UNEASILY, trying to place the noise that had disturbed her sleep. She listened for a moment, but the house held the stillness of early morning. Turning to a more comfortable position, arm stretching over the pillow, she struggled to recapture the dream that had seemed so pleasant. She heard the noise again. Her eyes, heavy with sleep, came open slowly. Jenny's face, inches away, confronted her.

"Go away, child. It's much too early. Go back to bed." Hester mumbled and closed her eyes again, but she could still feel the child's breath on her cheek. She opened one eye and tried to glare ferociously. Jenny giggled.

"Alice said I should come and fetch her when you're awake, and she'll bring you hot chocolate. Shall I fetch her now?"

"Yes, and you may tell Alice I shall likely give her the sack for allowing you to wake me up in the middle of the night."

Alice came in a few minutes later, and if Jenny had delivered the message, the maid appeared unconcerned, her mood as sunny as Jenny's. She hummed a little as she moved about the room, drawing open the draperies and raising the window. "Ah, Miss Hester, just smell that fresh air. A lovely day for a picnic. And wait till you see what Mrs. Mulliken has made for you and Miss Jennifer. Why, just walking into the kitchen and smelling all them good things cooking is enough to set a body's mouth to watering."

After one sceptical look, Hester ignored her. She sipped her chocolate and glanced through the letters Alice had placed on her tray. Jenny, sitting beside her, sipped her own chocolate, tilting her head in imitation of Hester.

Undisturbed by the lack of response, Alice continued to chatter. "Did you hear that fancy Miss Derringham is getting herself off to Paris? Now, that's a place I've a hankering to see one day, though I hear the food's not fit to eat."

Hester stared at her. "Where did you hear that?"

"From Mrs. Mulliken. She says those Frenchies cover all their food with such odd gravies and sauces that a body can't taste what he's eating. A waste is what—"

"I meant," Hester interrupted impatiently, "where did you hear that Miss Derringham was going to Paris?"

"Oh, that. Ben told us this morning. It's all over the village. Ben says she made a dreadful scene, yelling and throwing things until the old lord gave in and agreed to take her."

Hester glanced at Jenny, but she sat smiling, happily watching Alice, and didn't appear surprised or especially pleased by the news. Hester pulled one of her curls. "Did you hear that, Jenny? Miss Derringham is leaving the country."

"It doesn't really matter," Jenny replied with her grown-up air of gravity, causing Hester to wonder curiously just what had occurred at the manor yesterday.

Becky had heard the news as well, and as soon as Hester entered the breakfast room, she said, "I heard the most astonishing news. You'll never guess who's going to Paris."

"Miss Derringham?" Hester pretended to guess, as she took her seat. She laughed at the look of chagrin on Becky's face. "Alice was before you with the news."

"Humph. You'd think that girl had enough to keep her busy without spreading gossip all morning. Does she know what caused the Derringham girl to bolt? I wonder if it had something to do with Eversleigh. She almost ran me down in the hall when she was leaving the manor yesterday."

"Charlie's not going to marry her," Jenny piped up, and then quickly clamped a hand over her mouth.

"So that's the secret your brother told you yesterday, and why you were looking like a cat in a creampot," Hester teased.

Jenny couldn't help giggling. "But I wasn't supposed to tell anyone. Charlie said it was to be our secret."

"Never mind, Jenny. We won't tell Charles, and that shall be *our* secret. Agreed?"

Jenny nodded eagerly and politely asked to be excused. She had, she said, to go up and ready Mademoiselle for the picnic. Both ladies watched as she skipped from the room.

"I'm glad for the child's sake that Eversleigh finally had the sense to send that woman packing. Jenny's such a sweet child, she doesn't deserve to have that kind of sword hanging over her head."

"Really, Becky!" Hester admonished, with an apprehensive look towards the door. "We don't *know* that Eversleigh had anything to do with it. Hermione may have merely decided to refurbish her wardrobe."

Becky rolled her eyes up, and called upon Heaven to be her witness. "There are none so blind as those who will not see. I have never before had cause to believe you lacking in common sense, Hester. You cannot seriously believe that woman is leaving Eversleigh at your beck and call for the sake of a few new gowns?''

''Lord Eversleigh is *not* at my beck and call, and if you—''

''Excuse me, miss,'' Alice interrupted, holding open the door, ''Lord Eversleigh is here.''

Becky looked knowingly at Hester, who whispered angrily, ''If you dare say a word...''

''Good morning, ladies. It appears we have a fine day for our picnic. Where's Jenny? I fully expected to find her hanging on the doorstep, eager to be off.''

Hester smiled. ''You may be thankful that she spent the night here, or it would have been you she wakened at near dawn. She just ran upstairs to get her doll ready. I'm certain she'll return in a minute to hurry us along. Did you never take her on a picnic before?''

''No...not since our parents died. My mother loved picnics and she used to round us up whenever possible to spend an afternoon in the park. After she died, it just seemed too painful a reminder.''

Hester impulsively reached a hand to his. ''I'm sorry. I didn't realize...''

''Don't apologize. I should have thought of doing this before now. I can't recall the last time Jenny was so excited.'' He continued to hold her hand in his, and they both appeared lost in thought until Becky recalled them to their surroundings.

''If you'll excuse me, I must go and see if Mrs. Mulliken needs any help.''

Embarrassed, Hester hastily withdrew her hand, and Eversleigh grinned at the older woman, unabashed. ''You're coming with us, aren't you, Miss Becky? We must have at least one adult present.''

"Then you'll have to make do with Alice. Ben is driving Mrs. Mulliken and me into the village. We've shopping to do." Her voice was tart, but she eyed him fondly. He had that boyish look about him again, and passing his chair, she couldn't resist ruffling his hair.

He laughed and then teased Hester, "Will you feel entirely safe with only Alice and Jenny as chaperons?"

"Certainly, and you had best mind your manners. Alice has a much sterner notion of what's proper than Becky—even if she does seem to regard you as some sort of idol."

"No! Does she?"

"You needn't look so pleased. I'm sure any young man who was reasonably well looking, and who called at the orphanage where she was raised, would have been equally adored by her."

"The orphanage? Alice was reared there? I didn't know or I would have spoken with her. My grandmother was one of the founders, and after she died, my mother was very active."

Their conversation was curtailed as Jenny came bursting into the room, brimming with excitement. She recited a long list of all the edibles Mrs. Mulliken had packed, including a large ham bone for Blackie.

"Whoa." Eversleigh halted her, holding up a hand. "Who said Blackie was invited?" Almost as if he understood the words, Blackie trotted across the room and laid his large head on Eversleigh's knee.

"Please, Charlie," Jenny added her persuasion. "He needs the exercise, and it would be such a treat for him. Besides, he can help guard us in case any highwaymen try to hold us up."

"It's highly unlikely that we'll see any highwaymen. We're only going to our own park, you know. However, if Miss Hester agrees, then I'm plainly outnumbered."

With supreme confidence in her mentor, Jenny replied, "Oh, Miss Hester doesn't mind. He's her dog, after all."

Hester disclaimed any objections, and Eversleigh was teasing her on her preference for a dog's company when Ben tapped on the door. He came in, looking very grave and rather nervous. He coughed, stammered a little and finally managed to ask if he might have a word with Eversleigh. Jenny was dispatched to the kitchen to assist Mrs. Mulliken.

Ben stood just inside the door, nervously twisting his cap in his hands. "I thought I ought to tell you right away, governor. It's about the reward, in a way."

"Do you mean someone's come forward with some information?"

"No-o, not exactly. It's like this. There's this fellow named Clagg who heard about the reward. He thought it was rather odd you putting it up to find out about Logenberry, because another gentleman did the same thing about a year ago."

"Now this grows interesting. Have you talked to this man yourself? Where is he?"

The colour rose in Ben's face. "I had to go into the village this morning, governor, and well, you know how dusty that road is. I just stopped at The Crown for a minute or two to wet my throat, when this bloke approaches me. He'd been in the taproom asking about you, and Ned there told him he should speak to me."

"What exactly did he say, Ben? This could be important."

"Well, he says it was more 'an a year ago when this well-breeched cove sets it about that he'd pay well for a chance to chat with Logenberry. He didn't know the gentleman's name, but he gave me a good description of him. Clagg says he swore he meant Logenberry no harm. Just wanted to ask him a few questions. Clagg and Logenberry were friends, see, and he knew right off that it was Logenberry the gentleman wanted. So he goes and asks Logenberry what he wants he should do. The upshot was Clagg set up a meeting between this gentleman and Logenberry. Thing is, weren't long after that this Logenberry fellow up and disappears. Clagg ain't laid eyes on him since."

"Does Clagg know the identity of the gentleman?"

"He don't know his name, but he described him and I swear, governor, it sounded just like Master Stuart! Not only that, but Logenberry told Clagg that he met with him in a secret room, and I'll wager a shilling that's the room young Harry found."

"I shouldn't be at all surprised. I want to talk to this Clagg. Can you arrange a meeting? Tell him I'll be at The Crown this evening, and I'll make it worth his while to talk to me."

Ben nodded. "I'll be taking Becky and the missus into town this morning, and I'll just nip into The Crown then. Er, governor, I'd appreciate it if you wasn't to mention to the missus that I was there this morning. She takes a dim view of The Crown."

Eversleigh hid a smile. "We won't give you away, Ben. Just make certain Clagg is there tonight."

"Right you are, governor."

Hester, who had sat quietly during Ben's recital, released a sigh. "I do hope that if you persist in seeing that man this evening, you'll take Tobias or Zachary with you."

"I wouldn't want to scare him off. Besides, I don't believe there's any danger. This man was just a go-between. If you wish to worry over something, puzzle out why your cousin wanted to arrange a meeting with Logenberry."

Hester stood, sweeping her skirts around her. "From what I've learned about my cousin, he consorted with all manner of unsavoury characters. *You* worry over it while I find Jenny and fetch our bonnets."

Eversleigh appeared far from worried when she returned. He was in the courtyard, rallying Mrs. Mulliken over the size of the hamper she had packed. To Jenny's delight, he pretended to stagger under its weight as he lifted it into the carriage. When it was, at last, safely stowed, he hailed Hester. "Jenny's decided she should ride on the box with me, and you and Alice may share the carriage seats . . . with Blackie."

Jenny appealed to her. "If he were truly well, he could run along beside the carriage, but I don't think we should let him try that yet. He's still a little sore. You don't mind, do you, Miss Hester?"

"Of course not, Jenny," she replied sweetly. "Why ever should I object to having that mountain of a dog climbing all over my skirts, in the mistaken belief that he's a lapdog?"

"She's just funning," Jenny assured her brother. "She really likes Blackie."

Hester's fondness for the dog was put to a severe test, and she told him he should be thankful the ride was a short one. Within half an hour, Eversleigh drew his pair up in a clearing. The woods surrounded them on three sides; on the southern side stood a pretty brick pavilion overlooking a small lake. She had time to admire the lushness of the woods and the lawn sloping towards the water while Eversleigh tethered the horses and then helped Jenny down.

Blackie didn't wait for assistance. He leapt from the carriage in one bound and raced in circles, causing Hester to remark that anyone could see how ill the poor beast was.

Eversleigh grinned up at her as he extended a hand to assist her to alight and then helped Alice down. "I'll just put the hamper in the pavilion and then give you a tour."

Hester watched as he easily lifted the hamper and strode to the pavilion, Alice following faithfully in his wake. Jenny pulled on her arm. "Isn't it beautiful here, Miss Hester? Mama used to bring us here often."

"I can see why, Jenny. It's lovely. And how convenient to have a pavilion here."

"Mama had it built for us. Sometimes, if we were very quiet, we could sit there and watch the deer come out and feed at the lake."

"I'm afraid Blackie will discourage any deer. He's already scared away several of the pheasant. Perhaps you'd better go and get him, Jenny."

When Eversleigh returned, they strolled in leisurely fashion along the edge of the lake. Blackie barked at the water and then stuck a huge paw tentatively into it. He drew back, shaking his paw, and then tried to tiptoe through the shallow water. He kept them all laughing, and Eversleigh encouraged him. He tossed a stick just far enough in the lake to get Blackie's legs wet. The big dog would fetch it and bring it back to Eversleigh, eager for more play. The last throw went deeper, and the dog plunged bravely after it. Each surge forward sent the stick farther out, and the mastiff was completely soaked before he succeeded in catching it.

He bore it triumphantly back to shore and laid it before Eversleigh. Then, with a powerful ripple of his muscles, he shook out his coat, spraying the three humans with water.

Hester shrieked and dodged behind Eversleigh, and Jenny giggled as she took in her brother's glossy boots, now covered with water stains.

"Abominable beast! Go away!" He picked up the stick and flung it some distance, and Blackie raced off in pursuit.

"If Alice cannot remove these stains from my gown, my lord, I warn you I shall present you with a bill for its replacement."

"I fancy the boot's on the other foot, Miss Martingale. It was *your* dog who ruined these boots, and I shall hold you responsible."

"I always suspected you had no morals. That dog is mine in name only; his allegiance is to you, and if you like, I shall gladly make you a gift of him."

"What? And deprive you of such a wonderful watchdog?" He turned to gesture to the animal, but Blackie, heedless of their exchange, had trotted ahead to the pavilion. He was busily engaged in trying to convince Alice that he was on the verge of starvation and in dire need of sustenance. Jenny was pleading his case.

She succeeded in obtaining for him the ham bone, and Blackie immediately took it outside in the shade of the trees. When Hester and Eversleigh approached, he did not stop gnawing long enough to take notice of either of them.

"A watchdog, I believe you said? Give him a bone and Napoleon's army could march through here without his noticing."

"Unjust! This isn't his territory, and he knows us both. I'm certain that if we were at Silverdale, he'd be more vigilant."

"And I'm equally certain that he'd gladly accept a bone from any passing stranger who offered it and then grovel at his feet."

Jenny interrupted their argument by tugging on Hester's arm. "I can't find Mademoiselle. Wasn't she in the carriage with you?"

"Oh, Jenny. I don't remember seeing her. We must have left her at home in all the excitement."

Jenny looked ready to cry, and Hester hugged her. "Never mind. We shall have a lovely picnic, and you may tell Mademoiselle all about it when we return."

"It's not the same. She'll think I didn't want to bring her."

"Well, I think it's more likely that Mademoiselle didn't wish to come. She's very formal, you know, and probably wouldn't like dining alfresco."

Jenny brightened a little and agreed. "She doesn't like to get her dress dirty. I wager she hid from me so she wouldn't have to come." That settled, she proceeded to fill a plate till it was brimming over, and settled happily on a bench next to Alice.

Hester looked aghast at the amount of food laid out. "We'll never eat half of this. What a dreadful waste."

"If we don't, you'd best feed it to Blackie or risk hurting Mrs. Mulliken's feelings," Eversleigh warned her.

Alice was, at first, too shy of Lord Eversleigh to eat much. Noticing her reticence, he took pains to set her at ease, and soon had her laughing at his outrageous sallies. The afternoon passed rapidly, and it was one of the most pleasant Hester could recall. The weather had been perfect, and even now, she pointed out, there was only one dark cloud in the sky. Eversleigh looked where she indicated and then strolled outside the pavilion for a better view.

Hester joined him after a moment. "Do you think a storm is brewing? Perhaps we should start back?"

His brow was furrowed and his eyes narrowed against the sun's glare as he studied the formation. "Have Alice start getting our things together. I'm afraid that's smoke—and it's coming from Silverdale."

As soon as he said the words, Hester imagined she could smell the acrid odour of burning wood. Without another word, she turned and began to pack away the remains of the meal. Eversleigh brought the carriage round, and in a matter of minutes they were ready to leave. Blackie sat on the seat beside her, his nostrils quivering, and emitting a low, plaintive whine. Hester tried to soothe him as Eversleigh set the team to a fast pace.

The smoke grew heavier as they drew closer to home, and Hester could feel her heart pounding. The palms of her hands grew damp, and she pressed them against her skirts. Alice hugged Jenny against her, mumbling a prayer beneath her breath. When they rounded the final turn, they could see the smoke coming from the house in billowing waves. Ben was in the courtyard, directing several men passing buckets of water to fight the fire. His wife and Becky stood huddled near the hedge.

Eversleigh drew his team expertly to a halt and was on the ground striding towards Ben before Hester had fully realized they had stopped. "Stay in the carriage," he ordered tersely, his words floating back to her. But Hester was already climbing down. She held tightly to Jenny and with her other hand helped Alice to alight. The ladies hurried to where Becky and Mrs. Mulliken waited, ushering Jenny between them.

Hester released Jenny's hand long enough to hug Becky. "I'm so thankful you're both safe. When I saw the smoke—" She broke off, her voice choking on the words, and Becky hugged her again, patting her on the back.

"Don't cry, dear. I think the men have it fairly well under control, and the Lord be praised, no one was hurt."

Hester sniffed and drew back. "How...how did it happen?"

Mrs. Mulliken answered, "We don't know, miss. We were driving back from the village when Ben spotted the smoke. He set up the alarm right away. I don't think we've been back much above half an hour."

Becky nodded. "The men, bless them, came instantly. Ben thinks it started in the library, and they're concentrating on that. We could see the flames through the window as we came around the house. Thank God no one was inside."

"I suspect it was intended that way," Hester said angrily. She looked at the line of men, sweating profusely as they heaved the buckets of water, some coughing as the smoke fumes choked them. Eversleigh had replaced Ben at the head of the line, and she watched him for a moment. His shirt, already soaked with perspiration, clung to his back. She could see the muscles beneath working smoothly as he swung the bucket. She sighed, looking at her home. Her eyes travelled upwards to the second floor. There didn't appear to be much damage there yet. She knew the danger would come if the stairwell were to catch.

A flash at one of the windows caught her eye. She strained to see, shading her eyes from the glare. There was nothing there now, but she could have sworn she'd seen movement past the window.

Hester turned to ask Becky if she'd noticed anything, and suddenly realized Jenny was no longer beside her. "Becky, where's Jenny? Alice, have you seen her?"

"She was right here just a moment ago," Becky said. "She can't have gone far."

Hester trembled. She knew with dead certainty that Jenny was in the house. She recalled vividly how she had stood helplessly while her childhood home had burned, her parents trapped inside. Hester had struggled with a neighbour, desperately trying to fight free to get to her parents. They had held her back. She recalled the heat of the fire and the shouts of the men fighting it. They had yelled that the great stairway had collapsed, and then, with a giant rumble, the roof had caved in. Her parents had been trapped inside.

Hester hadn't cried. Not then. Not for her parents. Not for the cherished doll that had burned or the countless possessions they had lost. Everything her family had owned had perished in the rubble of the fire. Hester hadn't cried. Instead, she'd locked her anguish inside, and had suffered terrible nightmares for years afterwards.

She started towards the house, shrugging off Becky's arm. It would be too dangerous for any of the men to try the stairs. She was light enough, she hoped. She dashed in through the kitchen door and barely heard Eversleigh shout after her.

The kitchen was filled with thick, black smoke, and she could barely see her way. She used part of her pelisse to shield her face and moved as quickly as she dared. She was too afraid to call out to Jenny. A sudden noise might cause beams or the walls to collapse. The smoke was causing a harsh burning in her throat and eyes, and she tried holding her breath till she was out of the kitchen.

She entered the breakfast room. There, the heat was not quite as intense, but the smoke was heavy. She ran though, past the dining room and into the hall. At the far end, where the library was, she could see flames lapping at the door. Quivering with fear, she resolutely turned towards the stairs. She saw her then. Jenny was standing at the top of the stairs, holding on to the banister.

"Jenny," she called, her voice barely above a whisper, "hurry down."

The little girl stared straight ahead. With one hand, she clutched the doll tightly to her, and the other hand continued to hold the railing. Terror was in her eyes.

"Come down, Jenny. Hurry. I'll help you get out," Hester pleaded with her.

The child didn't move, and Hester realized she was paralyzed with fear. She uttered a prayer that the stairs would hold and gingerly made her way up. She had almost reached the top when a loud crack sounded, causing her to jump. It had sounded like a wall falling. Shakily, she grabbed the banister and as quickly withdrew her hand. The railing was already hot to the touch. Trembling now, heart racing, she climbed the last few steps and hugged Jenny. She had to pry the little girl's hand from the railing.

"Come with me, Jenny. It's all right now. I have you, sweetheart, and we're going to get out of here."

Jenny stood rooted, eyes staring vacantly. Desperately, Hester picked her up and started slowly down the steps. She tried to cover Jenny's face with her cloak, but it fell short. She turned the child so her face was hidden against her shoulder. Hester held her breath as she descended the last few steps and edged into the dining room.

Jenny was a dead weight, and Hester was breathing hard when they finally reached the breakfast room. "Just a few more steps,'' she told Jenny. They were within feet of the kitchen door when the flames shot through, collapsing the door inward. Hester fell back, cringing from the searing heat. In a panic, she tried to go back through the drawing room, but the fire had run along the woodwork there, and as she stood helplessly watching, the draperies caught fire and flared. They were trapped.

"God help us," she prayed, and looked around for any sort of protection. Her eyes fell on the cupboard, and for a second she thought she was imagining things. The cupboard doors flew open, and Eversleigh stepped out.

"Hester! Thank God," he breathed. "Quick, through here. Let me take Jenny." He lifted the child from her arms and half pushed her through the opening. Hester went down the steps blindly, almost tripping in her haste. The door to the courtyard stood open, and she stumbled out into the fresh air. Ben caught her as she fainted.

CHAPTER ELEVEN

HESTER WOKE LATER that evening, groggy and conscious of a mild headache, to find herself in an elegant bed-chamber. She had only the dimmest recollection of faint-ing and then regaining consciousness in Lord Eversleigh's arms. Or had she only dreamed that he had held her ten-derly before ordering someone to take her to the manor house?

The door opened quietly, and Becky's face peered round the door. Seeing that Hester was awake, she came at once to her side and took Hester's hand in her own. "How are you feeling, my dear? You gave us quite a fright today."

"Rather dazed. How's Jenny?"

"Thanks to you, she's just fine, although her hand suffered dreadful burns. I think I have aged ten years to-day. I feared we'd lose you both in that fire. That was truly a heroic thing you did. I know what it must have cost you to enter that house."

Seeing that Becky was on the verge of tears, Hester tried to make light of the matter. "If you truly love me, you'll fetch me a glass of water. My throat is dreadfully parched."

"Of course, dear. Now it's nearing eight o'clock. Eversleigh had dinner set back, and we're going to sit down shortly. Do you feel well enough to come down, or shall I have Alice bring you a tray?"

"I'll come down, but what has happened? Is the fire out?"

"We believe so, but Eversleigh left a couple of men there to keep an eye on things." She paused. "I'm afraid it's pretty bad, Hester. The kitchen was utterly destroyed, and the library gutted. Both the dining room and the breakfast room are in a dreadful condition. Truth be told, I'm amazed that the house is still standing."

Hester nodded, unable to discuss it. She needed time to think about what the loss of her home would mean. "I must look a fright. Let me up, Becky, and I'll see if I can't make myself a little more presentable before dinner."

Becky left her and she took stock of herself in the long mirror. Washing her face and pinning up her hair would help, but her dress was not only sadly wrinkled, but dirty and singed in spots. She was about to reconsider her decision and ask for a tray in her room, when Alice tapped on the door.

"Oh, Miss Hester. I'm ever so sorry about your house. Just when we were settling in so nice and all."

"Never mind, Alice. Let's just be thankful that no one was seriously injured."

"Yes, miss. And Lord Eversleigh has been so obliging. He had me freshen this gown for you, thinking yours must be a mess from the fire and all. Isn't it lovely? It belonged to his mama, and he thought you are about the same size. There's a whole closetful of her dresses and things in there," she said, gesturing to the door of the dressing room. She spread out a delicate satin gown of the palest ivory, embroidered with tiny green and gold flowers.

"It is lovely. Just the thing for a homeless orphan."

"No, Miss Hester, don't be talking so. You still have the land, and lots of folks who care about you. Especially

Lord Eversleigh. I've been suspicioning he'll ask you to marry him."

"Stop talking nonsense, and help me to change," Hester snapped at her with unaccustomed sharpness. She imagined everyone would be thinking Eversleigh would offer for her out of pity and misguided gratitude.

When Hester entered the drawing room, clad in Lady Eversleigh's becoming gown, pride stiffened her back and lifted her chin. She wanted no one feeling sorry for her. She need not have worried. Although she aroused many emotions in the two gentlemen present, pity was not among them. Dr. Layton hurried forward to greet her.

"I must be a better physician than even I believed to have wrought such a miraculous change. You look quite regal in that gown, Miss Hester. No one would guess what you've been through today."

She thanked him softly, and then it was Eversleigh's turn. His eyes held such a warm glow that the colour rose in her face.

"Not only is our lady heroic, but beautiful, as well. May I have the honour of escorting you to dinner?"

Embarrassed, Hester kept her eyes down but laid her hand lightly on his sleeve. She allowed him to lead her into the dining room, with Becky and Dr. Layton following. Eversleigh seated her solicitously, and she noted with surprise that the leaves had been removed from the table and places laid for only four.

"Where are the children? Becky said that Jenny was fine."

"She is, thanks to you, and wears her bandaged hand like a medal of honour. She and the boys are having dinner in the nursery with Miss Fontaine. They want to show Jenny how to eat with one hand. I fancy it will be a rather messy meal. And Richard is dining at the parsonage this evening."

"Jenny's a very fortunate young lady," Dr. Layton said. "If you hadn't acted so quickly this afternoon—"

"Please," Hester broke in, "don't say anything more. The truth of the matter is that I neglected Jenny. If I had been more watchful, she never would have entered that house."

"Say what you will, Miss Hester, but I insist upon drinking a toast to your health. And it's doubly thankful I am that we shan't be losing you."

Eversleigh shot him a wrathful look, and Hester peered at him, puzzled. He recovered quickly. "I mean you'll be staying on here for some time, of course. Charles told me he hopes you and Becky will be his guests until you can get your affairs sorted out."

"That's very obliging of you, sir," Hester told Eversleigh, "but we shan't impose on you for long."

"Impose? It's hardly an imposition. Actually, you will be doing me a favour. You're a wonderful influence on the younger ones, and you've brought me the best cook in the county, besides."

"A wonderful influence, indeed, when three members of your family are without the use of a hand, a fact for which I am, at least indirectly, responsible. As for Mrs. Mulliken, I know you're truly delighted to have her here, but your chef must be ready to give notice."

"Not him. I sent him off to the London house, which, I assure you, made him extremely happy. He never fully appreciated life in the country."

"You appear to have an answer for everything, and I do, truly, appreciate your kindness. But Becky and I will begin to look about for another cottage."

Eversleigh grinned, and she could not think what he found so amusing.

"I believe Miss Becky may have other plans," he said.

Becky blushed, and choking a little over her wine, stammered, "Oh, dear, I hadn't meant to tell you this yet, Hester. I wanted to wait till you...you've had such a shock today that I—"

"Becky, for heaven's sake, what are you trying to say?"

The older woman set her glass down and clasped her hands. Almost apologetically, she began, "I heard from Oliver Rundle this morning, and he...he has done me the honour of asking for my hand."

"Oh, darling, that's wonderful news. I'm so pleased for you." Hester motioned to Dr. Layton. "Now you may propose a real toast, and we can all drink to Becky's happiness."

"To our beautiful, blushing bride," he instantly obliged. "May she find true and lasting happiness."

They all drank while Becky sat, a shade embarrassed and laughing over their foolishness. "You're a bit premature, you know. I haven't given Oliver an answer yet."

"What? Keeping the poor fellow dangling, are you? And they say gentlemen are the heartless ones. What say you, Charles?"

Eversleigh lifted his glass in Becky's direction, giving her a mock salute. "I say Oliver Rundle is a most fortunate man."

Hester tried to join the good-natured teasing, but she was filled with apprehension. It seemed she was losing everything, even Becky's companionship. Her headache returned with a new intensity, and she prayed dinner would soon be over.

It was another hour, however, before Dr. Layton recollected that his wife would be waiting for him, and stood to take his leave. Eversleigh excused himself to see the doctor out, but was back within the space of a few minutes. Becky had gone to the kitchen to speak with Mrs. Mulliken and he found Hester alone.

"Hester, there aren't any words to tell you how grateful I am. If you had not rescued Jenny...well, it doesn't bear thinking about. I shall be forever indebted to you, and I want you to consider my home as your own. I hesitate to leave you on your first evening here, but I have that appointment in the village."

"Clagg! I had forgot him. Lord, was it only this morning that Ben told us about him? It seems an age since then." She didn't mention that the room they had spoken in was no longer habitable, or that she thought it was owing to the mystery of which Clagg was a part that her home had been burned. She didn't need to put it into words. Eversleigh read her thoughts easily.

"I know how you must be feeling. I think that somehow this all ties together, and the sooner we discover how, the safer you'll be."

"You think the fire was deliberately set?"

"I'm certain of it. Ben found some traces of rags stuffed in the shelves of the library. They appear to have been soaked in oil. I believe someone was only waiting for such an opportunity."

"Mansfield? I suppose we may rule out Lord Derringham. He's ready to leave for France, and I hardly think he'd do so if there were any evidence here linking him to a crime."

"Not unless he hoped to destroy the proof in a fire."

Hester looked startled.

"It's just possible," he told her. "Not probable. I'd wager my blunt on our friend Mansfield. I only hope Clagg can throw some light on this tonight." He hesitated and then added, "I realize you must be exhausted, but if you'd care to wait up for me, there's another matter I should like to discuss with you."

The warmth of his voice and the kind look in his eyes filled her with panic. "I...I don't know. I am rather tired, and I must see Jenny yet." She looked round, desperately seeking a diversion, and greeted Becky's appearance at the doorway with deep relief. "Becky, Lord Eversleigh is just ready to leave us. He's driving to the village to see that man."

Becky nodded, "Yes, I know. Ben asked me to tell you, sir, that he'll have the carriage at the door when you're ready."

Eversleigh studied Hester curiously, but he said nothing more, other than a brief good-night, before striding from the room.

Hester, almost giddy with relief, suggested to Becky that they retire to one of the sitting rooms. She plied Becky with questions about her plans with Oliver Rundle, and Becky, not loath to discuss her upcoming marriage, chattered on. Still, the hour came when the subject was exhausted, and Becky broached the matter of Hester's new situation tentatively.

"Of course, I shan't even consider marrying Oliver until I've seen you properly settled. I've been thinking of late that Lord Eversleigh seems taken with you. If he proposes, then you won't have to worry yourself over finding a place."

"I fear you mistake his emotion. It's only gratitude he feels, perhaps mixed with a little charity. When—if—I wed, it won't be merely for the sake of providing a roof over my head."

"Don't you find him the least little attractive, Hester?"

"Certainly. Lord Eversleigh is very...charming, but I want a marriage where there is...a mutual regard." She paused, searching for words, and then smiled. "I want a husband who will look at me the way Oliver looks at you."

"Was it that obvious?" Becky asked, pleased by the notion.

"Very. I'm only surprised he didn't speak before he returned to Town."

"He wanted to, but there was a matter that had to be settled before he was free to make me an offer. He explained it all in his letter. I can only say that it had to do with Lord Eversleigh, and although I can't betray his confidence by saying more, it has convinced me that Eversleigh would make you an ideal husband. Are you so certain he doesn't regard you in the way you wish?"

"I'm only certain that he feels a great deal of gratitude to me for rescuing Jenny, and now he seems to feel obliged to provide me with a home." Her chin came up. "I want neither his gratitude nor his pity. And, Becky, I don't want you worrying over this or letting it interfere with your plans. I shall manage quite well on my own."

"We'll discuss that when the time arises. Hester, I think perhaps you're letting your pride stand in the way of your happiness. If Eversleigh desires to marry you, for whatever reasons—"

"I'm sorry, Becky," Hester said, jumping up. "My headache has grown worse. You must excuse me." Before Becky could stop her, she swept from the room.

Hester ran up the stairs, dashing tears from her eyes that she did not wish Becky to see. She shut herself into her room, fearful that Becky might follow. She listened at the door, but there was no sound of footsteps in the hall. Hester resolutely wiped away the tears and crossed to the window-seat. The casement was open, and the night air felt cool against her warm cheeks and helped to dry the wetness.

She rested her head against the side of the enclosure and thought about Eversleigh. When she had found herself trapped by the fire, he had stepped through the cupboard in answer to her prayers. She might have denied it before, but in that instant, she had realized beyond doubt that she loved him.

She tried to consider her situation dispassionately. Eversleigh regarded her as the little governess next door, who had befriended his family and who had, inadvertently, saved Jenny. It was obvious that he now felt in some measure responsible for her. He had an exaggerated sense of moral duty. And now that she'd been left homeless by the fire and deserted by her one close friend, he would, no doubt, take it upon himself to provide for her. She was certain he intended to propose. He'd ensure she had a lovely home, and her every whim would be fulfilled. There was only one difficulty: she couldn't bear it. Couldn't bear him to look at her with pity in his eyes. Couldn't bear him to treat her with exquisite courtesy.

And she also had to consider Becky. She would not stand in the way of her happiness—on that she was determined. Becky deserved to have her own home, and someone to cherish her at last. Becky would protest, of course. But, for once, Hester didn't intend to listen. A stray tear trickled down her cheek, and she wiped it away irritably. Although she didn't realize it, the fire had taken its toll and had left her feeling extremely frail.

"Enough of this, Hester Martingale," she told herself sternly. "You've never been one to cry over spilt milk, so let's not begin now. You'll leave here just as soon as possible, and then send word to Becky and Eversleigh that you're perfectly content and well situated. Then they can get on with their lives.'' Another tear dropped forlornly as a knock sounded on the door.

Hester hastily dried her eyes and called a watery "Come in.''

Jenny opened the door and peered into the room. "Why are you sitting in the dark?"

"I was just watching the stars, Jenny. You can see them more clearly if the room is dark. Would you like to come and sit with me and look?"

Jenny padded across the room. She was in her nightdress, and her hair was freshly washed and just barely damp. She cradled Mademoiselle in her arms, carefully holding up her bandaged hand. Without another word, she climbed up on the seat in front of Hester, leaning back against her. Hester curled an arm round her, and Jenny sighed with contentment.

"I used to sit here with Mama, and she'd tell me a story. Do you know any stories?"

"Of course. Any governess worth her salt knows a story or two. Would you like to hear about the princess and the dragon?"

At Jenny's nod, Hester wove a tale about a beautiful princess, ultimately rescued by the handsome knight. She spoke in a low, soothing voice and felt the child growing drowsy. By the time the tale was told, Jenny was sound asleep.

Gently, she carried her to the bed. It wouldn't hurt Jenny to sleep with her tonight. Hester reasoned the little girl might suffer a nightmare over the fire, as she herself had done. She didn't want Jenny waking to a cold and empty room. She tucked her in, placing Mademoiselle on the pillow, and kissed her on the nose. She would miss Jenny.

Hester slipped quietly from the room, intent on finding Miss Fontaine. She feared the governess would be alarmed if she chanced to look in on Jenny and discovered her gone.

She found Miss Fontaine sitting with Becky in the drawing room. After assuring Becky that her headache was better, she told Miss Fontaine that Jenny was asleep in her room. The governess, pleased at an opportunity to chat with her, urged Hester to stay for a cup of tea. Unwilling to be alone with her thoughts, Hester remained. She let the woman's words wash over and around her, providing a distraction. They continued to talk until the candles were half burnt. Becky, growing sleepy, excused herself, and Hester, realizing how late the hour was, stood also.

The ladies were just leaving the room when Charles Eversleigh returned. He was both surprised and pleased to find Hester had not retired. He bade a hurried goodnight to Miss Fontaine and, taking Hester by the hand, drew her back into the room.

"Wait till you hear what Clagg had to say. The puzzle is almost solved."

Against her will, Hester found herself seated once more in the drawing room. Eversleigh paused only to bid Hodges to bring some sherry, and to stoke up the fire. Hester watched his lithe form, trying to memorize all the details about him to carry away with her.

"I do apologise for keeping you so late. We got immersed in this tale of Clagg's and forgot the hour. Still, I'll wager you'll think it worth losing a little sleep over." He sat beside her and poured a glass of sherry for each of them. Hester took the delicate glass, her fingers brushing against his, and found it difficult to focus on his words.

"First, I must tell you that Clagg is not the most reputable of fellows. I don't know what his lay is—I beg your pardon—I don't know how he makes his living, but one thing is for certain. He'll never agree to testify in a magistrate's court."

"He does know something, then?"

"Quite a bit. And combined with what we know, we were able to put the pieces together. Above a year ago, Stuart let it be known that he would pay handsomely to meet with a certain highwayman. He didn't know the man's name, but he had an excellent description of him. Clagg recognized it as his friend Logenberry and, seeing an opportunity for picking up a nice bit of blunt, set up a meeting."

"Are you sure it was Stuart?"

"Clagg knew who he was, all right. Your cousin spent a vast deal of time in the local tavern, and it was there, apparently, that he chanced to see Logenberry with our Lord X, as Becky calls him. Curiosity or natural deviousness made Stuart seek Logenberry out. He paid him well to divulge what his business had been with this peer. What he found out shocked even Stuart, and he demanded proof."

"Proof of what? You are the most exasperating man. What exactly did Stuart find out?"

"That Lord X hired Logenberry to waylay a certain lord and hold him up. Their scheme backfired. Their prey didn't submit tamely to being robbed and fought back. Clagg swears Logenberry fired only in self-defence, but his shot went home, and the lord was killed."

"Lord Mansfield! Rundle told me he was held up in broad daylight and shot. Louis Mansfield came into the title then. Do you mean it was *he* who hired Logenberry?"

"Yes, and your cousin was equally quick to deduce that, and to see the profit that could be gained from a touch of blackmail. Logenberry obligingly supplied him with the proof he needed before he disappeared."

"The evidence that Stuart wrote about, and that was supposedly hidden at Silverdale?"

He nodded. "Louis Mansfield was never of above average understanding. The fool sent a note to Logenberry telling him when the old lord was due home from London. And he signed it. Stuart bought the note, and then used it to blackmail Louis. Logenberry, incidentally, disappeared without a trace shortly afterwards."

"I suppose he was frightened away?"

"More likely Mansfield eliminated him, or perhaps your cousin. Clagg says he left a wife here, and she's not heard from him this past year. Even if he was on the run, he'd have got word to her in some way."

"This is even worse than I had imagined. Bad enough to have a blackmailer for a cousin, but a murderer? Are you certain you wish me to remain under your roof?"

"Very." He grinned at her. "You make this room infinitely more inviting." He reached to take her hand.

Unnerved, Hester quickly stood and walked a few steps away. "Well, what now? With Logenberry likely dead, and the only evidence burned, nothing can be proved against Mansfield. He has nothing more to worry about."

"Not quite. We have one advantage. Mansfield doesn't know we didn't manage to save that note, or that his dupe talked quite so freely to Clagg."

"But if Clagg won't testify—"

"He doesn't know that, either. Tomorrow I plan to pay a call on Lord Mansfield. Then we shall see."

She turned, alarmed. "Please don't. He's already responsible for his uncle's death and maybe Clagg's and Stuart's, as well. He'll stop at nothing."

"Now, don't fret. I think he'll realize the game is up." He rose and, standing beside her, gently touched her cheek. She saw the muscles in his jaw tighten and heard his voice grow hard. "I have a score to pay off with friend Mansfield. He put both you and Jenny in jeopardy. And I intend to see he pays for that."

"But perhaps the sheriff could—"

"No buts. I want you to retire now and get some rest. Tomorrow, we may have cause for celebration."

"Even if you should prove successful in this mad scheme, which I don't believe to be possible, I would scarcely consider it cause for celebration."

"No, how should you?"

"You said—"

"Never mind. You're overly tired. Come along, I promised Dr. Layton I'd see you got plenty of rest. So be a good girl and say good-night." He had walked with her to the foot of the stairs, and he stood watching as she slowly climbed the steps. Tomorrow would be time enough to discuss their future. In high good spirits, he set off down the hall, calling for Ben.

HESTER HAD INTENDED to wake early the next morning and to try again to persuade Eversleigh not to confront Mansfield. However, the long day had taken its toll, and the sun was well up when she woke. Jenny was already gone, and Hester feared Eversleigh might be, too. She rang hurriedly for Alice.

"Good morning, Miss Hester. Did you sleep well? I knew you'd sleep a little late this morning, what with not getting to your bed until the—"

"Please, Alice, not now. I must hurry and dress. Did you clean my walking dress? Has Eversleigh left the house yet?"

"No, miss," she replied, answering the last question. "He's downstairs in the breakfast room and don't appear to be in no hurry. He says I'm to tell you you'll find everything you need in the dressing room."

One of her problems was solved. When the double doors of the dressing room were opened, row after row of gowns and frocks appeared, along with shoes of every colour and a variety of those undergarments necessary to a lady. At another time Hester would have been in raptures over the beauty of the dresses. Now she merely reached for the first one and motioned Alice to help her into it.

Once gowned, she could barely contain her impatience as Alice brushed out her hair. "Never mind pinning it up—we can do that later. I must speak with Eversleigh before he leaves."

"Well, I never," Alice muttered, staring after her departing figure, but Hester was already gone.

She almost ran down the curving stairs. Seeing Hodges in the hallway below, she slowed her steps and contrived to greet him with a semblance of composure.

"Good morning, miss. You'll find his lordship and Miss Beckles in the breakfast room. This way, please." She followed his sedate pace, and took a deep breath as he held open the door.

Eversleigh stood as she entered and welcomed her with a warm smile. "Good morning. I can see that you slept well. You should always wear your hair down like that. It's very becoming."

Hester blushed, conscious of the footmen, and merely nodded to him before greeting Becky. She took her place at the table and accepted the cup of tea Becky poured for her.

"I hurried down because I feared you would leave before I had a chance to speak with you."

"My dear, after today you shall have all the opportunity you could wish to speak with me."

One of the footmen struggled to hide a grin, and Becky pretended an inordinate interest in buttering her roll.

"Thank you, my lord, but it is this morning that I wish to have a word with you." Mindful of the footmen, she continued, "I have been thinking over our discussion last evening, and I believe that your proposal to call on our friend is a serious mistake. It cannot possibly do any good, and perhaps a great deal of harm."

Lord Eversleigh tried to reassure her with his lazy good humour. "As much as it distresses me to do so, I must disagree with you on this one subject. But don't let it worry you. I shall return before you've had ample time to miss me."

"I won't miss you at all," she returned sweetly. "If you persist in this insane notion, then you leave me no choice but to go with you."

Maintaining his air of good humour for the benefit of their audience, Eversleigh rose and crossed to her chair. "I believe we should have a word in private. Will you join me in the library?"

"Very well, but you won't dissuade me."

Once in the library, with the doors securely shut, he faced her. "Hester, I cannot allow you to come with me. Surely you must realize that?"

"I realize that if Mansfield thinks you have him cornered, he'll fight like a rat!"

"And you would defend me?"

"Don't be absurd. I'm certain you are quite capable of dealing with another gentleman, but don't you realize how unscrupulous Mansfield is? He might very well shoot you in the back."

"Then I shall trust you to lay information with the nearest magistrate."

"Don't make light of this, please. I . . . I cannot allow you to place your life in jeopardy over this."

He moved closer and touched a curl lying against her neck. "I don't mean to tease you, and I'm touched by your concern. I don't believe there to be any danger, but on the off chance that Mansfield hasn't—well, I can't endanger you. I, on the other hand, must go. I am the Justice of the Peace, you know."

Hester felt her knees go weak and knew an urge to lean against his shoulder and simply agree to whatever he said. It took all her willpower to force herself to turn her back to him. "I'm not suggesting you ignore him, only let me go with you. Surely a witness must restrain him."

"I believe so."

She turned back to him hopefully. He took both of her hands in his and held her captive. "That is why I'm taking Ben with me. Hester, please, I beg of you, don't argue with me over this."

She read the implacable decision in his eyes. "Very well. I won't plague you any further. Now, if you'll permit me, I should like to finish my breakfast."

Hester did not return to the breakfast room. She went, instead, to her bedchamber. After ringing for Alice, she stood in front of the window watching the activity in the drive.

One of the stable lads had brought round the phaeton and was using all his strength to hold the pair of greys steady. Ben stood on the steps, apparently waiting for Eversleigh. No matter what he said, she could not allow him to do this. She could not bear it if anything happened to him.

"You wanted me, Miss Hester? Shall I do your hair now?"

"Not now, Alice. Please look in the dressing room and see if you can find me a suitable cloak and bonnet."

"Where are you going, Miss Hester? Do you wish me to come with you?"

"Thank you, no." Hester saw Eversleigh come out of the house. "Quickly, Alice. I must leave at once." The maid stood staring dumbly at her, and exasperated, Hester brushed past her. She found a cape that would serve and a wide-brimmed hat. Careless of her appearance, she jammed the hat on and, throwing the cape over her arm, hurried from the room.

"Tell Becky I'll be back soon," she called over her shoulder.

Hester chose to take the back stairs, and after racing through the kitchens with a wave to Mrs. Mulliken, she found herself in the kitchen garden. She thought the stables were to the left, and prayed Eversleigh had some sort of carriage or cart she could handle.

The giant who was guarding the stable area brought her up short. He stood well over six feet, with arms the size of small trees. Her eyes travelled up his frame to the massive head, and she noticed the peculiar break in his nose.

"Are you Zack?" she demanded. At his nod she commanded him to bring a carriage out at once. "You must come with me. I believe Lord Eversleigh is in danger. There's no time to be lost."

Zack, devoted to Eversleigh, needed no further urging, and Hester was surprised at the speed with which he moved. Minutes later, Zack furiously whipped the team he'd harnessed, and they careered down the drive.

CHAPTER TWELVE

"LORD HELP US!" Hester cried out as the road seemed to come up to meet them. They took the turn on two wheels and she closed her eyes against her fate. The far wheels came down roughly, jolting her against the seat, and her eyes flew open. They were on a straightaway now, and Zack cracked his whip, sending the horses flying. Hester strained her eyes against the sun's glare. For all their speed, Eversleigh was still nowhere in sight.

"Don't you worry miss. He can't be much ahead of us. We'll be there in a few more minutes."

"Zack! Watch out!" Hester screamed as another carriage came bowling towards them. She stared, half-paralyzed with fear as he whipped the team to the right, and they flew past the other carriage with only inches to spare. Zack's large hands hauled on the reins, barely slowing the plunging pair. They were on Mansfield's property now, and she knew the big house would be around the curve of the road, just beyond the woods. Hester could see the upper storey of the house through the dense trees. Abruptly they were in the clear, and she could see Eversleigh's rig in the drive and Ben walking the horses.

Zack slowed their carriage to a walk, and Hester was out, running across the courtyard to the entrance. She lifted the brass knocker repeatedly until the butler finally answered its summons. An elderly man, bent with age and half-blind, he peered out at her.

"Lord Eversleigh is here with your master, and I must see him at once. It's extremely urgent!"

The old man stared at her hat sitting crookedly atop her wind-blown hair, and knowing eyes deplored the dust layered over her cloak. "I beg your pardon, miss?"

"I said I must see Lord Eversleigh at once. Show me the way immediately. I told you the matter is urgent." With every second the man delayed, Hester expected to hear the sound of gunshots ringing through the house, and she reached out imploringly.

Perhaps it was the authority in her voice or maybe the demented look in her eyes, but the butler gave way before her. "Very good, miss. Follow me, if you please."

He led her up a long flight of stairs and then through an endless, narrow picture gallery where the Lord Mansfields of the past seemed to frown down at her unseemly haste. Hester ignored them, chafing at the interminable slowness of the old man. It seemed half an eternity before he finally paused in front of a wide oak door.

Hester swept past him and impatiently pushed open the door. She almost expected to see Eversleigh's body on the carpet and the corpulent Mansfield standing over him, gun in hand. The scene which met her eyes halted her in her steps, and she stood staring in silent disbelief.

Percival Mansfield, clearly at his ease, was stretched out on a lavish sofa. His slender fingers curled around a cigar in one hand, and a glass of amber liquid in the other. Staring at Hester, he blew a cloud of smoke, which seemed to hover above his head. Eversleigh, seated in the chair opposite, booted feet resting on an ottoman, appeared equally at ease. He glanced up in surprise. A hint of annoyance crossed his features briefly before he rose gracefully. "Ah, Miss Martingale. So you decided to join us after all."

Hester stammered an apology of sorts. "I didn't mean to intrude. I...it was only that I... Please forgive me. I...I needed to see Lord Eversleigh—"

The sound of booted feet pounding down the hall drew all eyes to the door. The butler, seeing a towering figure bearing down upon him, nimbly stepped to one side. He was not, after all, devoted to the Mansfields, and attempting to overpower a giant was clearly above and beyond the call of duty.

Zack ignored him and burst into the room, ready to do battle. He, too, came to an abrupt halt. His eyes travelled from Eversleigh to Percy, and then looked accusingly at Hester. Bewildered, he reproached her, "You said his lordship was—"

"Never mind that now, Zack," Hester was quick to interrupt. "You may wait for me below stairs."

Zack mutely appealed to Eversleigh, but at his nod, he reluctantly withdrew. The butler stared after him before quietly stepping out and shutting the door behind him.

Percy, with a broad gesture, invited Hester to be seated. "May I offer you some refreshment, Miss Martingale?"

"No, thank you," she answered, confused and embarrassed.

"I was just explaining to Lord Eversleigh how distressed I was to learn about the fire at Silverdale. It was...most regrettable. I am vastly relieved that you appear unharmed."

"I wonder if your father shares your sentiments," Eversleigh drawled.

"Oh, quite. I do assure you. He was extremely upset last evening. In truth, I feared that his heart might give out. If he were here, I know—"

"I don't wish to be rude, Percy," Eversleigh interrupted, "but where *is* your father? I sent word last evening that I would call upon him this morning."

"So he said, and I promise you he was quite inconsolable not to be here to receive you." Percy took out his fob watch and glanced at it. "Even as we speak, my dear father should be crossing the Channel. Once in France, our cousins there will arrange his transport to America."

"America!" Hester was stunned and turned to Eversleigh. He did not appear in the least surprised by this revelation. "Aren't you going to do anything?" she demanded.

"What would you have me do? Even if the authorities were able to apprehend Lord Mansfield in time, which I doubt, we have no proof to corroborate any charges."

"You arranged this, didn't you? You sent word last night so Lord Mansfield would have ample time to escape. You, a Justice of the Peace, aided a criminal. After all that talk last night about justice—"

"Here, now," Percy intervened. "Really, Miss Martingale. My father, for all his faults, is no criminal. It was all Bartholomew's doing."

"Bartholomew?"

Percy nodded. "Father's valet. Bartholomew was the one who suggested the scheme to waylay my great-uncle, and after the deed was done, he used it as a club over Father's head. Then Stuart somehow learned what had occurred, and began blackmailing my father. Did you know about that?"

It was Eversleigh who answered. "There was a notation in Stuart's diary that indicated he was blackmailing someone, and just before his death he wrote that he was doubling the price for his silence."

"Father was in despair. He was being bled by Bartholomew, and Stuart was demanding more and more. He sent word to Father that he wanted to see him. When Father got there, Stuart was alone. Father swore he never meant to kill him, but Stuart goaded him, doubling his price. Father raised his cane to him, merely threatening him, you know? But Stuart tried to dodge the cane and tripped. He fell and hit his head on the fireplace."

Percy paused and crossed to the sideboard. He poured himself a glass of sherry. There was complete silence in the room as he took a drink and then continued. "Bartholomew was furious when he learned what had happened. You see, he knew Stuart had proof of my father's involvement in his uncle's death."

"You mean the note your father sent to Logenberry telling him the date and time old Lord Mansfield would be returning?" Eversleigh asked.

Percy looked startled. "You found it, then?"

"No, only a confederate of Logenberry's who told us what the note contained. Logenberry sold it to Stuart."

"My father, alas, was not the most brilliant of men. He lost his courage when Stuart died, and locked himself in his rooms. Bartholomew took it upon himself to try to find the note. He knew his own life was not safe as long as that note existed. He broke into the house on the day of Stuart's funeral, but without any success, and again, the evening you arrived, Miss Martingale."

"Yes, Blackie heard him outside the window and scared him off. Was it Bartholomew who shot Blackie?"

"Regrettably, yes. That was when Father finally confessed to me." He shrugged and appealed to Eversleigh. "What could I do? Turn my own father over to the sheriff? I dismissed Bartholomew, of course. He could not implicate Father without incriminating himself, and I warned him I would see him dead if he tried.'' There was nothing of the mincing fop about Percy now, and his eyes glittered with a hardness that chilled Hester. She could well believe he meant what he said.

"I suggested Father try to buy Silverdale," Percy continued. "I believed I had the situation under control. If the note turned up before the purchase, I would deal with it somehow. Arrangements for Father's journey have been under way for some time. Unfortunately, I had not counted on Bartholomew. He was still lurking about, and when he heard of your decision not to sell, he took matters into his own hands. I am deeply sorry, Miss Martingale, for the loss of your home."

Hester brushed that aside. "What happened to Bartholomew? Do you know?"

"He's dead," Percy said in that cold, hard voice. "A falling-out of thieves, perhaps? I understand someone put a bullet between his eyes."

There was silence for a moment, and then Hester rose. "I scarcely know what to say to you, sir. Please excuse me. This has been rather a lot to... to comprehend."

Eversleigh rose to stand beside her, a hand on her arm. "I'm sorry it had to be this way, Percy. You could have come to me, you know. I might have been able to help."

Percy shrugged. "By the time I realized what was afoot, it was too late." He gestured to Hester, saying, "I regret... everything. Please believe me, my father never intended you any harm." He poured himself a liberal drink and added, "You shan't have to concern yourself with meeting me socially. I, too, am going abroad. Hermione begged me to join her."

Lord Eversleigh nodded and escorted Hester to the door. Once outside, she took a deep breath of the fresh air. He seated her solicitously in the carriage and then left her for a moment to speak with Zack.

Hester, shaken with relief that no harm had come to Eversleigh, was also mortified by her impetuosity in rushing after him. She blushed, thinking how her head-long flight must look to him. He had never stood in any danger and doubtless thought her a fool. Having cleverly manipulated Mansfield, now he probably thought to do the same with her, neatly planning her future. Well, Lord Eversleigh would soon learn she was not so easily led.

The drive back was accomplished in silence, each intent on private thoughts. They were nearing the manor when Eversleigh finally spoke.

"I know that this has been something of a shock to you, Hester, but now that the mystery of Stuart's death is finally settled, perhaps we can begin to plan our own future."

"Certainly, my lord," she answered tartly. "Why should you not plan *my* future? Are not we all puppets to dance to your direction?"

"Hester, what—"

"You weren't in the least surprised that Mansfield had fled. And why? Because you had planned it. You deliberately sent him a note warning him. And I don't know how you managed it, but you sent Hermione abroad, and now Percy, too. I think you've come to believe what people say of you. They all think you're some sort of demi-god around here."

"Hester—"

"Don't! Don't touch me. You may have manipulated the Mansfields, and even Becky and Rundle, but I, sir, am not one of your puppets. I won't dance to your tune, so you needn't concern yourself with my future." The look of hurt that crossed his features brought real tears to her eyes, and she fled the carriage as soon as it stopped.

When he came in, he could hear her light footsteps along the upstairs hall. His eyes followed the sound, half longing to go after her, and half despairing. Reluctantly, he turned away and made for the library. Hodges met him and was told, abruptly, to get out.

His butler retreated to the kitchen and confided in Mrs. Mulliken and Miss Becky that they were for it now. "The master's in there with the brandy decanter and doesn't want no one bothering him. He hasn't acted this way since his mama died. And Miss Martingale just went running up the stairs to her room."

Becky at once dried her hands and went in search of her charge. When she entered Hester's bedchamber, she found her lying face down on the bed, heaving great heart-wrenching sobs. She sat down beside her, and gently stroked her hair. "There, there, child. Cry as much as you please. You will feel better for it in the end."

It was Lord Eversleigh she was crying for, but Hester could not tell Becky that. She managed to check her sobs, and sat up. Becky's arm supported her, and she leaned against her old governess, much as she had done as a child. Choking a little over her words, she finally told Becky what had happened, painting Eversleigh as black as she dared.

"My poor darling. What a dreadful morning you've had."

"The worst of it is Eversleigh's arrogance. He thinks he has only to command and everyone will scurry to do his bidding. Who is he to decide what is best for everyone?"

"But Hester, surely it's better this way. No trial, no scandal. You would not want your cousin's name dragged through the courts. I feel certain Lord Eversleigh has done what's best for everyone.''

''I see he's got round you, too. Doubtless you and Oliver will wed to suit my Lord Eversleigh's convenience. Well, I, for one, will not be so easily manoeuvred.''

''Hester, this is nonsense you're talking. What did you expect Eversleigh to do? Why, he has extracted us all from a situation that could have been the talk of England, and spared you the disgrace of having your cousin's name on everyone's lips. I think he has behaved extremely well, and you, miss, owe him a debt of gratitude.''

Hester got up and walked to the windows. In her heart she agreed with everything Becky was saying, but she couldn't allow her to know that. She pretended an inordinate interest in the view. When she heard the door shut, she sank slowly onto the window seat. Just the thought of leaving the manor and never seeing Eversleigh again depressed her.

She recalled how strong and protective his arms had felt when he'd rescued her from Silverdale. He was wonderful, she thought. And he had handled the Mansfields brilliantly, without a breath of scandal. She couldn't help wondering what it would be like to be wedded to him. Then, shaking her head, she vainly tried to rid her mind of such an insane notion, and stood up briskly. Marriage was not to be considered. Any marriage of convenience would have been distasteful to her, but to be married to the one man she loved deeply, and know that he felt only compassion and pity for her, would be more than she could bear.

Pacing the room, she considered her alternatives. She wondered if Eversleigh would still want to purchase the Martingale land. If he did, that money, along with the income from her stock, would allow her to buy a small cottage somewhere—somewhere far away from York-shire. And then Becky could marry her Oliver, and everyone would be happy. Everyone but Hester Martingale.

Determined to ask Eversleigh before her courage failed her, Hester made for the door. She almost collided with Alice, as the girl entered holding a heavy tea tray. She helped Alice steady the tray.

"Lord, miss, that was close! You almost ended up wearing your tea. You weren't planning on going nowhere, was you?"

"Just down to speak with Lord Eversleigh for a few minutes."

Alice sniffed. "I'm sure it's not my place to say, but there's them below stairs what think I'm not a proper lady's maid, the way you go round looking like a cat drug in out of the rain! And if you do go down, looking the way you do now—"

Hester had a weak smile for her. "I've not been very considerate of you, have I? Very well, Alice. If you'll bring me some warm water, I'll try to get some of this dust off, and then you may dress my hair."

"Yes, miss!" Alice was gone before Hester could change her mind. While she waited, she studied her reflection in the cheval glass. No wonder her maid had been vexed. Her hair was in tangles, and a smudge of dirt decorated one cheek, streaked through by her tears. Her dress was filthy, and Hester quickly stripped it off. She had enough pride to wish to look her best when she faced Eversleigh.

While Hester was making her preparations, Eversleigh remained secluded in the library. He had made liberal inroads into the brandy decanter, and had almost reached the point where his conversation was no longer lucid. Dr.

Layton, knocking on the door, was told bluntly to stay the hell out.

"Now that's what I'd call a hospitable welcome for an old friend. Been hitting the bottle, have you, Charles?"

Eversleigh ignored him, and poured out two generous drinks, sloshing the liquid over the side of the glasses and onto the floor. "If you insist on staying, then shut up and have a drink. I'm not in the mood for any moralizing."

Dr. Layton accepted the proffered glass and studied his friend. He'd never seen Charles so dishevelled. His coat and cravat had long since been removed, and his white linen shirt wore several stains. It was open at the neck, and Charles had rolled up the sleeves. His hair, still unpowdered, was ruffled, and a rakish curl hung over his brow, giving him a devil-may-care look.

"Becky told me what happened, and for what it's worth, Charles, I think you did the right thing."

Eversleigh looked at him through bloodshot eyes, trying to decipher what the doctor was talking about. "Oh, you mean about Mansfield. Well, I'm glad *someone* approves. You should have a chat with that bloody governess upstairs. She finds my methods high-handed and overbearing."

"Hester? What are you talking about?"

Neither Eversleigh nor Dr. Layton, intent on their conversation, noticed Hester quickly enter the room. She had heard the last bit of their discussion and now stood silently, waiting to hear his answer.

"She took exception to... to my methods. Thinks I manipulate everyone. I don't know, Layton. Time was when I thought I knew women fairly well, but she has me at a loss. She's not like any other woman I ever knew. One minute I can believe she almost cares for me. But the next, she acts as if I were some sort of monster. 'Course, that's not unusual for her. It's been that way since we first met...."

"Give her time, Charles. What with the fire, and then the shock of finding out about Mansfield, she's been through rather a lot. I'm sure when she's had time to think things through, she'll come to see how wisely you acted."

Eversleigh shrugged. "I doubt that. I've done everything I could to help her, and she doesn't appreciate it. Not one bit. And not only that, she even suspected me of doing in her cousin."

"And what else was I supposed to think?" Hester, angry now, stalked across the room and faced Eversleigh. "The first day I met you, you'd just come from my solicitor's office, and then you practically threatened me."

"Threatened you? Now where did you get that idea? I've never threatened you. Doctor, see to Miss Martingale. I fear she's suffering from delusions."

"You did! That first day at Silverdale. You said that if I remained there against your advice, my life might be in danger."

"For God's sake, Hester, that wasn't a threat. Even then I was concerned for your safety."

The doctor had a suspicion things would go better if he weren't present, and he edged quietly towards the door and slipped into the hall. He needn't have worried. Hester and Eversleigh were too involved in their argument to be aware of either his presence or absence.

Hester stood before him, hands on hips, and Eversleigh tried hard to concentrate on her words instead of his wish to pull her roughly into his arms.

"That may have been your intention," she was saying, "but it wasn't the impression you left. Even so, I'd begun to trust you until you removed that book from Stuart's room without telling me. And when I asked you about it, you acted so strangely that I started having doubts again.''

''I gave you back the blasted book.''

''Oh, yes. After several pages had been removed.''

He had the grace to look ashamed and mumbled something.

''I beg your pardon, my lord, but I cannot understand if you insist upon slurring your words.''

''I said I ripped out the pages deliberately. I was hurt you wouldn't take my word that it was of no importance.''

''And then you wonder why I don't trust you? Of all the stupid, childish things to do.''

''Maybe so. But Rundle trusted me, and Becky. I didn't think it was too much to ask of you. Could you not have relied on their judgement?''

Hester looked away from his penetrating eyes, but Eversleigh would not allow it. He moved a step closer, and with one hand lifted her chin up so that she faced him. ''Was that too much to ask of you?''

''They... they were blinded by your charm.''

''Ah, and obviously *you* were not,'' he sneered, turning away.

She wondered if she had only imagined the injured look in his eyes. ''Someone had to think rationally. And you admit you gave me cause to wonder—''

''And did you also think I deliberately shot Blackie? Or hired thugs to waylay my own carriage? Or shot my own brother?'' he interrupted harshly.

''No, of course not. By that time I was fairly sure you weren't involved. And then, when you found those stocks for me, I knew for certain you couldn't have had anything to do with Stuart's death.''

Eversleigh gave a queer laugh and walked away from her. He refilled his glass and saluted her. "The only thing ever lied about, and that convinced you to trust me. How perfectly ironic."

"What are you saying? What did you lie about?"

"Nothing. It doesn't matter now."

"It does. You must tell me. It was something to do with my stocks. What? If you won't tell me, I'll get it out of Rundle."

"I told you, it's of no importance now."

"Of course not, if *you* say so, my lord. Who could gainsay you? I had quite forgot that you are omniscient."

Furious with her, goaded beyond endurance, he shouted, "Have it your own way, Miss Martingale. *There were no stocks.* There, does that satisfy you?"

Hester stared at him. "No stocks? But what of the cheque Rundle gave me?"

Eversleigh was tired, and the steady drinking had taken its toll. He no longer cared what happened, and told her bluntly. "It was my idea. I bought the stocks in your name and convinced Rundle to go along with me. Don't worry, the stocks are yours. You'll always have the income. Consider it a gift for saving Jenny's life."

"Why on earth would you do such a thing?"

He had turned his back, and she barely heard his answer. "I didn't want you to leave. I imagined the stocks would give you enough income so that you could stay at Silverdale."

"Another bit of your high-handedness, my lord? It didn't suit you to have me leave Silverdale yet, so you simply arranged a suitable income for me? Your audacity knows no bounds, sir. How dare you presume so? Why didn't you want me to leave? Did you need me as bait i your little charade to trap Mansfield?''

Her words brought him spinning round to face her, fu in his face. Hester felt her heart beating rapidly as he too hold of her arms. His face was only inches from her ow Almost afraid to hear his answer, she asked in a whispe ''*Why?* Why would you pretend such a thing?''

She bent like a slender reed against his strength, and h lips came down on hers, hard and bruising. One of h hands became entangled in her hair and held her hea firmly beneath his lips. She closed her eyes, giving he self up to his kiss. She almost fell as he abruptly put he aside and crossed the room.

Hardly daring to breathe, Hester followed him. He voice soft and hesitant, she put the question again.

His back was to her, head bowed, and it was difficult t hear him. Hester strained to catch his words. ''I didn' want you to leave. I had some insane idea that if yo stayed at Silverdale, I might convince you to...to...''

She gently touched his shoulder, turning him to fac her. ''Convince me of what?''

He saw the warmth in her eyes and felt the tender touch of her fingers, and groaned. ''Hester...I've been in lov with you for so long. I thought that if you remained a Silverdale, I might have a chance with you. Can you for give me for—''

She threw her arms about his neck, almost knockin him off balance. ''Charles! Oh, Charles!'' Her lips foun his, and for long minutes they forgot everything else When he finally released her, she murmured, ''I though you were going to propose because I saved Jenny. Just ou of gratitude. Tell me again that you love me.''

More than a little hazy from drink, he wasn't sure wha had happened, but he had her in his arms, and he wasn' about to let her go. "I love you. I think I have loved you since that first day I saw you." One finger gently traced the line of her jaw, and then her lips before he possessed them again. If she needed any further proof of the depth of his feelings, she found it in a long and passionate kiss.

He released her a little, and she looked up at him, her heart in her eyes. A tiny hand reached up to caress his face, and Charles took a deep breath.

There was a commotion at the door, and they turned as one. Dr. Layton came in, followed by Hodges, bearing a tray. "I thought some coffee might be in order," the doctor said, unabashed. Looking at them standing together, Eversleigh's arm still round Hester's waist, he added, "*Now* may I congratulate you?"

His friend, with an idiotic grin, nodded. "You may, at least I think so." His arm pulled Hester closer. "You did just agree to marry me, didn't you?"

Hodges so far forgot himself that he actually smiled, and was moved to say, "My lord, Miss Martingale, the staff will be *most* pleased to hear this news."

"Thank you, Hodges. Would you please ask the children to join us, and Becky, also?"

Dr. Layton prepared a cup of much-needed coffee for Eversleigh and handed Hester a glass of champagne. "I've been waiting days to drink a toast to you. Thought Charles would never get round to asking you."

Hester laughed, but her answer was lost to the din in the hallway. Jack was the first to run in and demanded excitedly, "Is it true, Miss Hester? Are you really going to marry Charlie?"

"Yes—" she laughed, "—but how did you know so quickly?"

"Alice told us," Harry answered, coming forth to extend his hand. "We're very happy for you and Charlie, miss," he said, standing on his dignity. "And if you war to send us all away for a spell, we'll understand."

Even Jenny had been wakened, and she dodged in fron of him. "Miss Hester won't send us away. She likes us don't you?"

Hester knelt and hugged the little girl. "I love you darling, and besides, I have always wanted to be part of large family."

Richard was next in line, and hesitantly kissed her o the cheek, telling her quietly, "I'm very glad he had th good sense to choose you." Charles, feeling a little lef out, demanded his due. "Why is Hester receiving all th congratulations? *I* did all the work."

"And took your own sweet time about it, too," Beck chided him before pulling him down and placing a nois kiss on his rough cheek. She hugged Hester then, and had to wipe a trace of tears from her eyes. "I couldn't wisl better for you, my dear, and Oliver will be so pleased."

"Yes, and you may tell him I've a bone to pick witl him. Telling me my stock came from Uncle Cyrus whe all along it was Charles's doing. Did you know, too Becky?"

"Only recently. Oliver wouldn't confide in me becaus your young man there swore him to silence. But he fi nally told me." Seeing the militant look in Hester's eyes she added quickly, "I wouldn't have allowed him to do such a thing, but he told me how much Eversleigh wante to marry you."

"A fine thing this is," Hester said to her intended "You seem to have told everyone but me."

"Even Mademoiselle knew," Jenny piped up. "But i was a secret because Charlie said you didn't like him above half."

They all laughed, and the scene in the library began to look more and more like a party. Several of the staff came in shyly to offer their felicitations, and Mrs. Mulliken brought in several trays of her famous pastries.

It was hours before Hester had a minute alone. She managed to slip out with Jenny, and took the tired little girl up to bed. As she bent over to tuck her in and kiss her good-night, Jenny gave her an especially warm hug. "Good night, Mama," she whispered softly.

Hester was deeply touched, and went along to her bedchamber with a light step. She wanted to freshen up a bit before returning to the library and Charles. *Charles*. Just saying his name gave her a special thrill.

THE CANDLES HAD BURNT LOW, and the embers were dying in the fireplace, but the newly engaged couple continued to sit contentedly side by side. Eversleigh murmured in her ear, "I truly think I fell in love with you the first time I saw you."

"What? At Silverdale when I had just arrived in all my dust and dirt? And I thought you were a man of discriminating taste."

"You looked charming then, with all the children gathered about you. But I meant that first day in Rundle's office when you looked me up and down so boldly."

Hester blushed at the memory and snuggled closer in his arms. "I didn't think you recognized me. You have never mentioned it."

"Not recognize my own heart and soul? I knew in an instant that you belonged to me."

Hester couldn't help laughing, spoiling the moment. "Come now, my lord, confess. If you were truly omniscient and could have foreseen all the trouble I would cause you, you would have fled the country."

"Not at all," he said, gathering her close again. "Not when I knew the day would come when I could sit here with you in my arms."

"I think you prevaricate, sir, but I'm much too content to protest overly much."

"Protest all you wish, dear heart. I believe I've found a way to silence you quite effectively."

"Really, my lord, I..." Her voice trailed off as he smothered her words with his kisses.

Outside the large double doors of the library, Hodges was still on duty, guarding his employer from any intrusion. He thought he heard Miss Martingale speak occasionally, but oddly enough, she never did seem to finish a sentence.

PENNY JORDAN

Sins and infidelities...
Dreams and obsessions...
Shattering secrets
unfold in...

THE HIDDEN YEARS

SAGE — stunning, sensual and vibrant, she spent a lifetime distancing herself from a past too painful to confront... the mother who seemed to hold her at bay, the father who resented her and the heartache of unfulfilled love. To the world, Sage was independent and invulnerable— but it was a mask she cultivated to hide a desperation she herself couldn't quite understand... until an unforeseen turn of events drew her into the discovery of the hidden years, finally allowing Sage to open her heart to a passion denied for so long.

The Hidden Years—a compelling novel of truth and passion that will unlock the heart and soul of every woman.

HARLEQUIN

Romance®

**This September, travel to England
with Harlequin Romance
FIRST CLASS title #3149,
ROSES HAVE THORNS
by Betty Neels**

It was Radolf Nauta's fault that Sarah lost her job at the hospital and was forced to look elsewhere for a living. So she wasn't particulary pleased to meet him again in a totally different environment. Not that he seemed disposed to be gracious to her: arrogant, opinionated and entirely too sure of himself, Radolf was just the sort of man Sarah disliked most. And yet, the more she saw of him, the more she found herself wondering what he really thought about her—which was stupid, because he was the last man on earth she could ever love....

Harlequin Intrigue ®

Trust No One . . .

When you are outwitting a cunning killer, confronting dark secrets or unmasking a devious imposter, it's hard to know whom to trust. Strong arms reach out to embrace you—but are they a safe harbor . . . or a tiger's den?

When you're on the run, do you dare to fall in love?

For heart-stopping suspense and heart-stirring romance, read Harlequin Intrigue. Two new titles each month.

HARLEQUIN INTRIGUE—where you can expect the unexpected.

Harlequin Superromance®

Available in Superromance this month
#462—STARLIT PROMISE

STARLIT PROMISE is a deeply moving story of a
woman coming to terms with her grief and gradually
opening her heart to life and love.

Author Petra Holland sets the scene beautifully, never
allowing her heroine to become mired in self-pity. It
is a story that will touch your heart and leave you
celebrating the strength of the human spirit.

Available wherever Harlequin books
are sold.